Tina flattened her palms against his chest so she could push him away.

Do it! her conscience ordered. *Give him a shove and tell him to go home.*

I will, Tina reassured herself. *Any second now. Yes, sir. I'll call a halt to this ridiculous game we're playing.*

Only, she didn't. There seemed to be a short circuit in the communications between her will and her body. There she sat, practically stupefied, while a man she cared about prepared to make his second terrible mistake. The first had been their first kiss. The second would be more of the same. Unless she stopped it.

The weak protest she finally managed to make wouldn't have been enough to deter anyone who didn't respect her. Fortunately, Zac did.

He got to his feet and backed away from the swing. "Oh boy," he said, a bit breathless. "We have to stop meeting like this."

Books by Valerie Hansen

Love Inspired

The Wedding Arbor #84
The Troublesome Angel #103
The Perfect Couple #119
Second Chances #139
Love One Another #154

VALERIE HANSEN

was thirty when she awoke to the presence of the Lord in her life and turned to Jesus. In the years that followed she worked with young children, both in church and secular environments. She also raised a family of her own and played foster mother to a wide assortment of furred and feathered critters.

Married to her high school sweetheart since age seventeen, she now lives in an old farmhouse she and her husband renovated with their own hands. She loves to hike the wooded hills behind the house and reflect on the marvelous turn her life has taken. Not only is she privileged to reside among the loving, accepting folks in the breathtakingly beautiful Ozark Mountains of Arkansas, she also gets to share her personal faith by telling the stories of her heart for Steeple Hill's Love Inspired line.

Life doesn't get much better than that!

Love One Another
Valerie Hansen

Published by Steeple Hill Books™

STEEPLE HILL BOOKS

ISBN 0-373-87161-9

LOVE ONE ANOTHER

Copyright © 2001 by Valerie Whisenand

Visit us at www.steeplehill.com

Printed in U.S.A.

A new commandment I give unto you.
That you love one another; as I have loved you,
that ye also love one another.
—*John* 13:34

To all the wonderful people in my life
who are so easy to love, especially my husband,
children, grandchildren and special Christian
friends. And to the one person I find it so hard
to forgive, for being the way the Lord has chosen
to show me that I'm not perfect...yet.

Chapter One

❧

Tina Braddock bent over a low table, up to her elbows in green and yellow finger paint and up to her knees in preschool tots. It was fortunate the colors blended with her floral print skirt because Sissy Smith had a handful of the fabric and was tugging vigorously.

"Miss Tina! Miss Tina!"

"What is it, Sissy? Is your picture finished?"

The little blond girl ignored the question. "Miss Tina, look! A *stranger*." She used both gooey hands to gather up the loose edge of her teacher's apron and try to hide behind it.

Straightening, Tina looked toward the door. Her breath caught. Sissy was right. The man standing there *was* a stranger. The best-looking one she'd seen in longer than she could remember. His hair was brown and his eyes were so dark they were almost black. As if that weren't enough, the good Lord had blessed him with about six feet of height and a stature that insisted he could pick up a small automobile all by himself and fling it across the room without even breaking a sweat.

Tina blinked herself back to reality as she smiled a greeting. "Hello. Can I help you?"

"I didn't mean to scare the kids," he said soberly. "I just came to look the place over before I enroll my son."

She extricated herself from Sissy's grasp, tossed her long light brown hair back over her shoulders without touching it, and crossed to him while wiping her hands on her apron. "I'm Tina Braddock."

As he eyed her greenish-yellow fingers he hesitated, so she withdrew the offer to shake hands. "Oops. Sorry. I tend to forget. Not everyone gets as involved in all this as I do."

"I can believe *that*."

When he smiled down at Tina, the whole room suddenly seemed a hundred times brighter. "I'll be glad to put your son on our waiting list. How old is he, Mr....?"

"I'm Zac Frazier," the man said. "Justin's just turned four."

"Oh, good. We should have several openings in the four-year-old group in a month or so, as soon as school starts and some of my Picassos-in-training go on to kindergarten."

"That's not soon enough."

"I beg your pardon?"

"I just moved here and I need a place for my son right away. I thought you understood that."

Tina remained firm. "Our rules are for the good of all the children here. Perhaps a private baby-sitter?"

"I can't do that." Frustrated, Zac raked the fingers of both hands through his thick, wavy hair. "Justin gets panicky if I leave him alone with adults. He's better when he's with kids his age."

That's odd, Tina thought. Children usually got upset when they were thrust into a group of unfamiliar kids, not when they were privy to an adult's undivided attention.

"The more distractions, the better he seems to do," Zac said. "That's why I thought…"

The handsome daddy seemed to be having trouble deciding whether or not to explain further, so she encouraged him. "Why don't you tell me a little about your son's background, Mr. Frazier?"

"There's not much to tell. Like I said, he's only four." Zac cleared his throat. "His mother died last year, when we lived up in Illinois. Since then, he hasn't wanted to let me out of his sight."

"Ah, I see." Tina quelled the urge to reach out and comfort him with a sympathetic touch. "I'm so sorry."

"Yeah, well…" He stuffed his hands into his pockets and struck a casual pose. "So, will you take him?"

"I can ask my boss. I suppose one more—"

Across the room, Sissy yowled. Tina whirled just in time to see redheaded Tommy McArthur upend a dish of yellow poster paint over her head. The thick goo pooled in her curls, then began to ooze over her forehead and trickle down her face.

"Tommy!" Racing back to the art table, Tina held out cupped hands to try to catch the worst of the mess.

Sissy chose that moment to shake her head like a kitten whose nose had been dunked into a saucer of milk. Globs of yellow pigment flew. Several caught Tina in the face. She was sure she could feel others clinging to her long hair.

The rest of the children backed away, wide-eyed and uncertain. Except for Sissy's ongoing wails, silence reigned. The boy who had caused the ruckus dropped the empty paint dish as his lower lip began to tremble.

"Hold still, Sissy," Tina said firmly. "You're just making things worse."

"My dress!" the little girl howled, looking down at her skirt. "My mama sewed it for meeee..."

"I'll wash it out for you and it'll be good as new. I promise. Just stop shaking your head!" Tina had momentarily forgotten Zac Frazier. Then she heard him start to laugh. The sound was warm and full. It filled the room and made the hairs at her nape tickle. Goose bumps stood up on her arms.

She glanced over her shoulder at him. "There are

towels in that cabinet up there,'' she said, cocking her head to indicate. "Top left. Mind handing me one?''

"You sure one will be enough?'' Zac was still chuckling as he moved to comply.

"Let's hope so.'' Tina was trying to keep from bursting into giggles and upsetting Sissy even more. "I'd get it myself but I seem to have my hands full.''

"No kidding.'' He stopped behind her and passed the towel over her shoulder. "Here you go. Anything else I can do for you while I'm handy?''

She was concentrating on wiping Sissy's face and sopping up the worst of the paint in her hair. "Like what?''

"Oh, I don't know. Hose the place down, maybe?'' He crouched beside Tina and solemnly eyed the red-haired boy who'd started the trouble. "Or maybe you'd like me to dunk this guy in a different color for you?''

Tina gave Tommy a stern glance, then smiled at Zac. "Sorry. As tempting as it sounds, I'm afraid they don't let me paint naughty children, even if they do deserve it.''

"What a shame,'' Zac said, straight-faced. "He'd look great in purple.''

"We'll have to settle for an apology, instead,'' Tina said, playing along. "Tommy, what do you have to say to Sissy?''

"She started it!'' the boy wailed. "She splashed green on my shirt.''

"Okay. That does it. Painting time is over," Tina ordered. She straightened and wiped her hands on a relatively clean corner of the towel. "Everybody to the sink to wash. Sissy first. March."

Zac stood, too. "You sure you've got a handle on them?"

"As good as I ever do," she answered, smiling fondly as her small charges headed for the low sink in one corner of the room. "They're really good kids. They just have a lot to learn about getting along with others."

"So do the kids I work with...and they're considerably older."

"Oh? Where do you work?"

"Over at the high school, starting next week," Zac said. "I'm going to substitute teach when I'm needed but I'll mostly be a guidance counselor."

"Well," Tina said, grinning up at him, "that sure will simplify things around here."

"It will?"

"Uh-huh. Once you get established in your job at Serenity High, all we'll have to do to spot the teen-age troublemakers is look for the ones you've painted purple."

Tina was glad her boss, Mavis Martin, was the kind of woman who listened to reasonable suggestions. She'd waited until all the children had gone home before approaching her and explaining about wanting to add Justin to her class.

"I suppose it's okay, if you're sure you can cope," Mavis said, nodding her graying head soberly. "If it was me, I'd probably do the same thing. The poor man obviously needs help. Might as well come from us, don't you think?"

Smiling broadly, Tina nodded. "Absolutely. Bless you. You're a dear." She reached into the pocket of her apron for the card with the phone number of the motel where Zac and Justin were staying. "I'll call Mr. Frazier and tell him his son can start tomorrow."

"Okay. I just hope you aren't biting off more than you can chew. What kind of kid is he?"

"I don't really know much about him, other than what I was told. He's supposed to be overly attached to his father but adjusts better when he has other children as a distraction."

Mavis's forehead puckered in a frown. "You mean you didn't meet him today?"

"No. His daddy came by alone."

"Hmm. What do you suppose he did with Justin when he came to look us over?"

Tina was beginning to see why her boss seemed troubled. "That's a good question. Let's use the phone in your office so I can put it on speaker and you can hear, too."

"That's not necessary. I trust your judgment."

I wish I could say the same, Tina thought. But she couldn't. Being too trusting, too gullible, had cost her plenty in the past and would have ruined her future, too, if she hadn't left everything behind and started over where no one knew her.

Mavis followed her into the cluttered office. "Push aside my stuff and make yourself a place to sit down, honey. I keep meaning to get this place straightened up. I just never seem to find enough time. One look at all this and I give up because I know it'll take too long."

"My mother used to say cleaning up a big mess was like eating an elephant. It can't all be done at once. You have to take it one bite at a time."

"Well, well, well," the thin, middle-aged woman drawled, staring at Tina in amazement. "You've worked for me for over a year and that's the first time you've mentioned your family. How is your mama?"

"She passed away a long time ago," Tina said softly. Thoughts of the past had obviously caused her to let down her guard. That mustn't happen again. Once she started telling her story she'd run too great a risk of inadvertently revealing her secret shame.

"I'm so sorry to hear that," Mavis said. "Is your daddy still living?"

"No." The answer sounded crisp and off-putting, much to Tina's distress. She didn't want to be unkind, especially not to a friend and mentor like Mavis Martin, but she didn't intend to discuss any aspect of her prior family life. Not now. Not ever.

Looking for a distraction, she quickly dialed the

motel and asked for Zac's room. He answered on the first ring.

"Hello?"

"It's me, Tina Braddock, Mr. Frazier. I've talked it over with my boss, and I'm calling to invite you to bring Justin to meet me and the other children. Is tomorrow morning too soon?"

She was sure she heard a relieved sigh.

"No. That will be fine. What time?"

"If you come around ten, he can start by having milk and cookies with us."

"Good. We'll be there."

Mavis was waving at her and making hand signals from across the desk. Tina got the idea. "One question, if you don't mind?"

"Sure. Shoot."

"You said Justin didn't like to be away from you, right?"

"Right."

"So where was he today when you came by the day care center? Why didn't you bring him with you?"

"Ah." Zac let out his breath in a whoosh. "I guess that might seem odd if you didn't know the whole story. We'd been awake most of the night. He was sound asleep when I left. I figured it would be better to be by myself when I scouted out places for him to stay, so I let him sleep."

"You didn't leave him in a motel room all

alone?'' She couldn't believe a father who had seemed so concerned would have done such a thing.

''Of course not. I paid one of the maids to baby-sit. Justin never even knew I was gone.''

''Oh. Thank goodness. I thought...''

''Look, Ms. Braddock,'' Zac said tightly. ''I'm doing the best I can under the circumstances. I'd like to spend every minute with my son, but I can't. I have to work. That's why I need a place like yours to take care of him during the day. The rest of the time he's my responsibility. One I take very seriously.''

Instead of attempting to justify her position, Tina fell back on her professional demeanor. ''I'm sure you do. I certainly didn't mean to imply otherwise.''

''Sorry.'' Pausing, he muttered to himself before continuing. ''It's not your fault. I know I get defensive sometimes. It just galls me that so many people don't think fathers are capable of taking good care of their kids by themselves.''

''All anyone can do is try,'' Tina told him. ''No two children are alike. Sometimes, even a person's best efforts aren't good enough without the help of divine intervention.'' *Like she'd gotten with Craig.*

''You sound like an expert,'' Zac said. ''Do you have children?''

Touched by the irony of his question, she gave a soft, self-deprecating chuckle. ''Dozens. All other people's. And I'm certainly no expert. At least, not once they get older than about six. I'd rather face an unruly gang of twenty preschoolers than try to figure out one teenager.''

"Boy, not me," he countered. "I don't envy you your job one bit. Give me a reasonable teen any time.''

"There is no such thing as a reasonable teen," Tina argued amiably. "Believe me, I know.''

"That sounds like the voice of experience. We'll have to compare notes sometime. Maybe I can give you a few pointers and you can do the same for me.''

"I'll be glad to help you and Justin in any way I can. See you tomorrow, then. Bye.''

Curiosity filled Mavis's expression as Tina hung up the phone. "I thought your specialty was little tykes. You never mentioned that you'd worked with teenagers.''

"I haven't." Tina busied herself straightening piles of paper on the desk rather than continue to meet her boss's inquisitive gaze. She'd slipped again. That was twice in one day, which was two times too many. "I was just making polite conversation.''

"Oh." The older woman reached out and stilled Tina's fluttering hands. "If you don't stop rearranging my papers, I won't be able to find a thing. Go on home. I'll lock up.''

"You're sure?" Tina was eager to leave, to be alone where she could sort out her thoughts and gain better control of her tongue.

"I'm positive." With a motherly smile, Mavis looked her up and down. "You deserve a break.

You've either had a particularly rough day or a truck full of raw eggs crashed into you while I was busy in the other room.''

Tina laughed lightly. ''The yellow spots are from finger paint, not egg yolk. Tommy got mad at Sissy, and the rest is history. I was kind of caught in the middle.'' Recalling the funny incident, she shook her head. ''To make matters worse, it happened exactly when Zac decided to drop in to look the place over.''

Mavis's left eyebrow arched. ''Zac?''

''I meant Mr. Frazier,'' Tina said, blushing.

All her boss said was ''Of course you did.''

Justin Frazier was a miniature version of his daddy. The minute she saw the lonely little boy, clinging tightly to his father's hand, Tina's heart belonged to him.

She made sure all the other children had their cookies and milk, then approached father and son. ''Hello, Justin. My name is Miss Tina. I have an extra cookie that really wants to be eaten. Do you suppose you could help me with that?''

He buried his face against his father's pant leg.

''Okay,'' Tina said casually. ''I guess I can give it to one of the other boys if you don't want it. That wouldn't be really fair, though. They've already had theirs. I saved this cookie specially for you.''

Justin rolled his head just far enough to reveal one dark eye, and peeked out at her.

"It's chocolate chip. Of course, if you don't like that kind…"

One pudgy hand reached out. Tina quickly handed him the cookie and turned to rejoin the class, subtly motioning Zac to follow. "How about a carton of milk to go with that?"

Without looking back, she proceeded to get the milk, insert a straw and set the carton at an empty place at the low table as if she fully expected Justin to agree to sit there. "Here you go. Nice and cold."

For a moment it looked as if he was going to continue to hang on to Zac in spite of Tina's assured manner. At the last second he let go and slid into the scaled-down plastic chair. None of the other children said a word. They were all too busy studying the new arrival and his daddy.

Across the table, little blond Emily began to giggle, when Justin bit into his cookie and half of it crumbled and fell on the floor. Tina was about to offer him another, when she saw Tommy McArthur carefully break his own cookie in half and lean closer to hand the piece to Justin. She was too far away to hear what the boy said, but she figured it had to be funny because Zac had his lips pressed tightly together and was struggling not to laugh.

To her relief, Justin accepted the gift and whispered something back to Tommy before stuffing the whole half of the cookie into his mouth at once.

Zac stepped back quietly. As soon as he was far

enough away, Tina joined him. "What did Tommy say?" she asked.

Shaking his head for a moment to compose himself, he said, "I think my son just took his first bribe. He promised Tommy he'd see that I didn't dunk him in any paint."

"No wonder you looked like you were about to burst!"

"I was surprised he even remembered me. I told you I didn't understand little kids."

"Hey, don't worry about it. Nobody really does. They don't even understand themselves."

"You sure seem to know how to handle them, though. I was worried Justin would pitch a fit when I tried to let go of him. It was amazing he didn't."

"I think sometimes we underestimate the adaptability of children. All I did was act like sitting at the table with the others was the most natural choice for him to make, and he made it. It's that simple."

"For you, maybe. When I told him he was going to day care this morning, he threw a terrible tantrum. It's a wonder the folks at the motel didn't hear him and call the police."

"Have you found a house, yet?" Tina asked, keeping watch on the children as she talked.

"No. And I'm getting pretty frustrated."

"Well, as long as you don't throw a tantrum..."

"Very funny. Although I did feel like it yesterday when we drove seven miles out of town to look at a place and found out it was already rented."

"In a close-knit area like Serenity, most of the best places never get advertised. People just hear they're going to be for rent or for sale, and tell their friends."

"Terrific."

"It has its advantages. For instance, I happen to know that the house two doors north of me is going to be vacant soon. It's in a nice neighborhood and only about a quarter-mile from the high school. Would you be interested?"

"Interested? At this point I'd practically kill for a decent place to live."

Tina laughed. "I don't think you'll have to do anything quite that drastic. I'll talk to the folks who are moving as soon as I get home tonight and find out all the details for you. Hopefully, there won't be too long a wait."

"You'd go to all that trouble for me? Why?"

Looking up into his eyes, she saw how much her kindness had affected him. This was a man who apparently wasn't used to experiencing the honestly offered concern of strangers. Or accepting their help. He was never going to fit in around here if somebody didn't set him straight. Tina immediately decided it was her duty to be that person.

"In small communities like this one, Mr. Frazier, folks help each other all the time. It's how we are. We don't need specific reasons to look out for one another. We just do it. A lot of us behave that way because Christians are supposed to, but we aren't the

only ones who show kindness. Pretty much everybody does. It's one of the blessings of living here.''

"I see."

Tina decided to press ahead. "Do you have a
church home? If not, you can't beat the one I go to,''
she said enthusiastically. "We'd love to have you
visit this Sunday. At nine-thirty I teach a Sunday
School class of children Justin's age. He should be
comfortable enough with me by then to enjoy it.
Regular church starts at eleven."

"We'll see." He glanced at Justin. "I guess I
might as well try to get out of here. I do have a lot
to do."

Tina scanned the table where her charges sat. "I
think you're wise to leave him with us right away,
instead of getting him used to having you stick
around. He'll be fine. Just go over and tell him goodbye as if you've done it that way a thousand times.
I'll take care of the rest."

"What if he cries?"

"Then, I'll give him a hug and comfort him until
he stops, the same as you'd do," she said. To her
dismay she noticed that the man seemed a bit put off
by her comment. Surely he didn't expect a mother-
less child to do without a lot of cuddling, even if his
father didn't view it as a natural masculine response.

"You do whatever you think is right," Zac said.
"You can reach me at the high school all afternoon
if you need me. What time should I come back for
Justin?"

"We like to lock up and be out of here by six-thirty. Will that work for you?"

"I'll make it work," he said.

Tina watched him walk stiffly across the room and bend over his son. The boy didn't seem at all upset when he bid Zac goodbye. Funny. She'd dealt with lots of little ones in the past and she'd expected at least a mild protest, especially since Justin hadn't had time to make friends yet.

Hanging back, she waited for the boy's reaction rather than anticipating difficulties and telegraphing her own concern. If he accepted his father's departure, there would be no reason to treat it as anything but routine.

Zac straightened and headed for the door. He never hesitated, never looked back. If Tina hadn't spotted the moisture glistening in his eyes as he passed, she might have believed he wasn't concerned about leaving Justin at all.

Chapter Two

Tina wasn't surprised that Zac was the first parent to claim his child that day. It was barely four-thirty when he arrived. Justin looked up from the rug where he was pushing a toy race car, broke into a wide grin when he spotted his daddy and ran to him.

Zac tousled the boy's thick brown hair. "Hi, buddy. Did you have fun?"

Nodding, Justin suddenly turned shy again and hid his face against his father's leg, just as he had that morning when he'd first arrived.

Troubled by the abrupt change in the child's attitude, Tina approached. "You'll need to sign him out on that clipboard hanging on the wall by the door. Just find his name, fill in the time and sign in the space provided."

She followed, as Zac took the boy's hand and led him toward the door. Justin was dragging his feet and not looking at anyone, so she crouched down beside him as Zac paused to check the pupil list.

"It was very nice having you in my class, today, Justin," she said amiably. "Tomorrow we're going to paint, and play with the outside toys and have lots more fun."

When the boy looked into her eyes, Tina was positive she saw a glimmer of fear. She gently stroked his bare arm to soothe him. "And then tomorrow, after school, your daddy will come for you again. Just like he did today." Still not sure she was getting through to the little boy she added, "And I'll be your special friend. If you want to keep me company while I walk around and do my job, you can be my helper, okay?"

"O-okay." His voice was barely above a whisper. As soon as he spoke he looked up at his father for reassurance.

Tina, too, looked up. "I think you should tell Justin that it's okay for me to be his friend," she said. "He seems worried that you might not approve."

"He doesn't need a friend Ms...."

"It's Braddock, remember? But call me Miss Tina. Everybody does. It simplifies things for the children."

"All right. My son needs a teacher and a caretaker, Miss Tina. That's why I brought him here. However, I don't see how becoming emotionally involved will help you do a better job. Or help Justin adjust to the new routine."

She blessed the little boy with a smile of encouragement before she straightened to face his father. The smile faded and her chin jutted out. "Everybody needs friends, Mr. Frazier. Even stubborn, hardheaded men like you, whether you choose to admit it or not."

"Ah, I see. Are you volunteering?"

Tina didn't like the self-satisfied expression on his face. Her eyes narrowed. "Why do I get the idea that's a trick question?"

"Because it is. You aren't the first single woman who's figured she could get to me by befriending my son," Zac said flatly. "And I'm sure you won't be the last. I learned a long time ago that it was best for Justin if I put a stop to that kind of nonsense before it got started."

"You think I'm pursuing you?"

"It's pretty obvious."

"Oh, really?" Righteous indignation rose. "Well, let me tell you something, mister. If I was interested in getting to know you on a personal level, which I am *not*, I'd have the backbone to come right out and say so, not hide my intentions at the expense of an innocent child."

Zac was starting to smile for real. "Are you through?"

"No." She pulled a pout. "But I think I'd better stop talking before I say too much."

"Undoubtedly. I suspect I may have to rethink my conclusions about you."

"I certainly hope so."

"In that case, I apologize, Miss Tina." He politely offered his hand. "If you want to be buddies with my son and can keep me out of the equation, then I certainly have no objection."

That's big of you, she thought cynically. For the boy's sake she took Zac's hand, intending to shake it merely to demonstrate harmony. It should have been a simple act. It wasn't. The moment he grasped her fingers some serious complications arose. Tina felt a jolt of awareness zing up her arm and spread telltale warmth across her cheeks.

A barely coherent "Thanks" squeaked out of her suddenly tight, dry throat as she quickly withdrew from his touch. No wonder he'd had so much trouble with other women! The poor guy was unconsciously sending out the wrong kind of signals. At least, the ones she was picking up were wrong. *Very* wrong. Especially for her.

Zac cleared his throat. "So, what time can I bring Justin in the morning?"

"We open at eight. I'm usually here by a little after seven, if you want to drop him off early. You'll need to knock. I keep the door locked when I'm here alone." The cautious look returning to his eyes reminded her of the conversation they'd concluded a few moments before, so she clarified her statement. "I will *not* be waiting with baited breath for you to come in with him."

Chuckling, he nodded and relaxed. "Okay, okay. I'm convinced. You're not shopping for a husband."

"You've got that right."

"Mind telling me why not?"

Tina's stomach tied in a hard knot. She *did* mind. A lot. But it wouldn't do to say so and start an unnecessary discourse. She hadn't even told her brother Craig, back home in California, what had convinced her to stay away from romance no matter what else happened. There was no way she was going to explain that kind of personal trauma to a stranger. Especially since her past history had been the obvious reason for at least one failed relationship.

"It's not relevant," Tina said, choking back any sign of emotion. "Let's just say I'm perfectly happy with my life as it is. I live in a great town, and having these wonderful kids around me all the time blesses my socks off."

"Ah, so you're happy with the status quo. Me, too. Too bad the rest of the world doesn't understand that, isn't it?"

"Do eligible women *really* chase you around all the time?" she asked, baiting him on purpose to take his focus off her life and put it back on his.

"Yes." Zac laughed softly. "Actually, that was one of the reasons I decided I needed to move to this tiny corner of Arkansas. My friends meant well, but they were fixing me up with dates so often they were driving me crazy."

"My boss, Mavis Martin, is like that." Tina

pointed to an adjoining room. "She takes care of the littlest babies over there in our nursery. She means well, too, but sometimes…"

"Don't be too hard on her. She probably wants to make sure you're not lonely." Zac paused, thoughtful. "In my case, Justin and I are doing fine as we are. We're a team." He glanced down at the boy and tousled his hair again. "Aren't we, buddy? Well, tell Miss Tina goodbye for now. You'll see her again in the morning."

Crouching to be on the boy's level, she touched his free hand and smiled with fondness. "Bye, Justin. I'll see you soon."

For an instant the boy leaned her way, and she thought he was going to break down and hug her. Instead, he whispered, "Bye," and hurried to keep up with his daddy as Zac started for the door.

Tina's heart went out to the child. Zac Frazier might be a whiz at understanding the older kids he worked with, but he had a long way to go before he met all the emotional needs of his four-year-old son. Somebody was going to have to show him the error of his ways soon, or the boy was likely to carry the scars of the lack of physical closeness all his life.

It was painfully clear to Tina that she'd been placed in a perfect position to enlighten him. The trouble was, she didn't feel even remotely qualified for such a daunting task.

"Oh, Father, why me?" she prayed softly. *"I couldn't even straighten out my own brother. How*

*am I ever going to show that man how to love his
son the way he should?''*

No easy answer came. She didn't expect it to.

It was over a week before Tina had any news for
Zac about available housing. The trouble was, the
only house she'd found was the one close to hers.
Too close. She wrestled with her conscience all day,
knowing she should give him an update about it and
hating to because she didn't want to have to deal with
him as a neighbor. Nevertheless, she gave in and
presented the address when he came to call for Justin.

"This is the rental I told you about," Tina said.
"If you haven't found a place yet, this one is going
to be vacant soon. The landlord wants to have a
chance to clean it up and paint it before he rents it
again, so I'm afraid you'll have to wait a while."
Shrugging, she said, "Sorry. It was the best I could
do."

"How about if I volunteer to do the painting to
save time? I really don't want to keep Justin in that
motel any longer than I have to. It's not enough like
a home."

"I agree. He told me a lot of his toys are in storage
and he wants to be able to get the boxes out and play
with everything. He rattled off a list of treasures that
had the other kids drooling."

"*My* son told you all that?"

"In great detail. He has a very good vocabulary

for a child his age. I suppose that comes from spending so much time with adults.''

"The only adult he has much to do with is me,'' Zac said. "And you, of course. He talks about *Miss Tina* all the time. I think he has a crush on you.''

She laughed lightly. "That's pretty normal, too. I can't help but get attached to these kids and they respond to me the same way. I love 'em all. Even Tommy.''

"The kid I was going to paint purple?'' Zac chuckled. "I remember. Is he still acting up?''

"From time to time. He's a healthy boy. He can't help some of the things he does, like not sitting still or not remembering to keep his hands to himself. But he's improving. They all are.''

"Even my son?''

The man looked so concerned, she decided to go into more detail. "Justin has never caused me any trouble. Actually, that much virtue had me worried to begin with, but I've been watching him, and he's beginning to act more normal. I've actually seen him getting into a little mischief lately.''

Zac stiffened. "I'll have a talk with him.''

"No!'' Tina was so adamant she forgot herself and grabbed Zac's forearm, holding tight. "Don't you dare. That would spoil everything. He's just starting to loosen up and have fun here.''

Casting a wary glance at her hand where it gripped his bare arm, Zac said, "Looks like he's not the only one who's loosening up. Your fingernails are leaving dents. If I promise to behave myself, will you let go of me?''

''Oops. Sorry.'' Embarrassed, Tina jumped back. It would be a hot day at the North Pole before she touched that man again! She didn't have to look in a mirror to know her cheeks were bright pink. So was her neck.

''You're forgiven. It's nice to know you care so much. About Justin's welfare, I mean.'' He cleared his throat. ''By the way, that's a great color on you.''

Brushing her hands over her skirt, she said, ''This? Thanks. I chose it because the paint spots blend right in.''

Zac was clearly amused. ''Actually, I meant the color on your face. Have you always blushed so easily?''

''Only when I forget myself and grab hold of strange men,'' Tina responded with a nervous laugh. ''Believe me, it doesn't happen all that often.''

''Let's hope not.'' Looking across the room, he beckoned to his son. ''Come on, Justin. We're going to go look at a house before dinner.''

The little boy raced to his dad. ''A *real* house?''

''Yes. A real house. See?'' Zac showed him the paper with the address on it, then looked over at Tina. ''I forgot to ask. How do we get there?''

''It's not hard. You take the main highway west, past the market and up the hill, then veer right at the first road after the vacant lot where Ed Beasley used to keep all those rusty antique cars.'' She was waving her hands for emphasis.

''Who?''

Frustrated, Tina realized they had a basic information problem. ''Never mind. I forgot. Ed sold out and moved before you came to town. I usually navigate by familiar landmarks, which is a good thing since the dirt roads around here don't have street signs posted.''

''Could you draw me a map?''

''I have a better idea.'' She glanced at the wall clock. ''If you can wait another twenty minutes, I can lead you there myself. That way you won't get lost. When I first moved here I took a wrong turn on one of those unmarked roads and I thought I'd *never* find my way back to civilization.''

''So, the house is stuck way out in the country? I'm not sure that's what I'm looking for.''

''Unpaved streets do not mean it's rustic,'' Tina countered. ''You'll see. It's a lovely house. And the yard is fenced so you won't have to worry about Justin wandering off when he's playing outside.''

Zac was shaking his head. ''That's not a problem. My son always stays where he can see me and I can see him, when we're at home.''

It was his matter-of-fact attitude that gave Tina pause. No normal child of four kept an eye on his or her parent every minute. It wasn't natural. Or healthy. Zac Frazier was a smart man, an educated man. Why couldn't he see that?

Or was it just that he didn't want to?

* * *

Zac hung around until the last of the children had been picked up, then he and Justin followed Tina out to the parking lot. He'd pictured her as the convertible or the sports car type. Instead, she floored him by climbing into an old, dusty, blue pickup truck.

He secured Justin in his seat in the rear of their minivan and got behind the wheel. Hopefully, he hadn't looked too surprised at Tina's mode of transportation. He didn't want to hurt her feelings when she was trying so hard to do him a favor.

She pulled alongside, windows rolled down. "Ready?"

"Lead the way," Zac called.

As soon as she drove off, he turned up the van's air-conditioning. Ahead, he could see Tina's long, light brown hair blowing in the wind. She might not be driving a fancy new convertible, but he hadn't been far wrong about her overall attitude. She looked exactly like the free spirit he'd been picturing ever since they'd met.

No wonder she wasn't interested in settling down and getting married. She wasn't the sweet, contented homemaker type Kim had been. Thinking of his late wife gave Zac a familiar jolt of guilt. He'd been over and over the boating accident in his mind and had never come up with a clear cause, yet his subconscious kept insisting it was his fault. It had to be. After all, he was the husband and father. Keeping his family safe was his responsibility. And he'd failed. By the time he'd pulled Justin to safety and gone back for Kim, she'd sunk below the surface of the murky water and he hadn't been able to locate her.

Ahead, Tina signaled for a turn. That snapped Zac out of his contemplative mood. He was glad she wasn't speeding, because he wouldn't have compromised Justin's safety just to keep up with her. His days of risk-taking were over.

The road narrowed beneath a canopy of trees. Scraggly, dead tree branches stuck out here and there on both sides of the road like long, crooked fingers. If it had been dark, the scene might have seemed eerie. As it was, however, the lovely summer day lingered to bathe the countryside with rays from the setting sun. Lush growth on the healthier oaks and cedars softened the angles of their bare counterparts.

Checking Justin in the mirror, Zac saw that the boy had already fallen asleep. Good. The poor kid needed the rest. He sighed. Truth to tell, so did his daddy. Between the two of them, they'd spent many restless, nightmare-filled nights this past year. Maybe a new house, a new town, a new job were what they needed. Zac certainly hoped so. He was running out of fresh ideas.

Tina pulled into a driveway and parked. Zac followed, and couldn't believe his eyes. He stared. There were flowers everywhere. Hundreds of them. In pots, in planters, coming up in bunches in the lawn. He'd never seen anything so naturally beautiful in his life.

Climbing out of the van, all he said was "Wow."

Tina joined him in time to hear the comment. "I'm glad you like it. Gardening is a hobby of mine."

"This is your place? I thought…"

"Sorry," she said, pointing. "The one you came to see is three doors down. I turned in here by force of habit. Guess I was daydreaming. Come on. We can walk over."

Zac cast a weary glance at his sleeping son. "I hate to wake him. He has a lot of trouble getting to sleep."

"Then, leave him alone and move your car over in front of the other house where we can watch him. I'll meet you there."

She started off without waiting for him to agree. Watching her go, Zac was struck by her effortless grace and lively step. Always before she'd been inside the classroom when he'd seen her move. Now, she'd shed her shoes and was cutting across the lawn barefoot, like a child who'd just been let out of school.

What a fascinating woman. There was an easy goodness about her that spoke to his soul, made him miss the spiritual aspects of his former life. Maybe it was time to take her up on her invitation and make plans to visit her church. If even half the members were as amiable as Tina Braddock, it was a place he wanted to see for himself.

* * *

"The Nortons left their key under the mat so you could get inside," Tina said, handing it to him. "Here. Go take a peek. I'll stay out here and watch Justin for you."

"You're sure they won't mind?"

"Nope. They've moved most of their furniture already. Doris told me to give you the key and turn you loose."

"She's not worried about letting a stranger poke through her home?"

"You're not a stranger," Tina told him. "I vouched for you. Besides, the Norton's oldest boy is in high school, so they've already heard plenty about you."

Zac arched an eyebrow. "Small-town gossip?"

"You'll get used to it. Everybody means well. They like to keep an eye on newcomers, that's all."

"How long does it take to become one of the good ole boys?"

Tina laughed. "A couple of generations, as near as I can tell. A genuine southern accent helps, too. I'm working on mine."

"I thought I'd noticed a drawl in some of the quaint expressions you use."

"I'm not adding colloquialisms on purpose," she explained. "They slip into my conversation because I hear them so much. When I first moved here, I used to always catch the unusual ways people talked. Now, it's hard to pick up differences even if I'm listening for them."

"Not for me," he said, laughing quietly and shaking his head. "The other day one of the teachers I work with said he was 'fixin' to take a cold,' and I had to stop myself from asking him where he was planning on taking it."

He fitted the key into the lock and turned it till he heard it click. "Keep a close eye on Justin. I had to leave the motor running so the air conditioner would work. If he wakes up and sees I'm gone, he'll be scared. This shouldn't take long. I'm not fussy."

"Don't you worry one bit. I'm not fixin' to leave till you're as happy as a possum in a henhouse," Tina quipped, grinning widely.

Zac rolled his eyes and turned away, laughing to himself. The woman was naturally humorous, whether she knew it or not. No wonder Justin had taken to her so quickly and blossomed in her class. Tina Braddock was more than a good teacher. She was a very special person, too.

Chapter Three

Concerned about safety, Tina strolled toward the van while she waited for Zac to return. She understood why he'd chosen to leave the motor running. Justin needed the cool air. The weather was typical of summer in the Ozarks: steamy and hot, good for flowers and veggies but not as pleasant as it would be in a month or so when fall arrived.

She shaded her eyes and peeked in the van window. Justin was asleep on the bench seat in the center, close enough to the driver to be watched, yet protected from the front air bag. It didn't surprise her that Zac had chosen the best location for his son. The man didn't miss a trick where safety was concerned.

The boy stirred. Holding very still, Tina willed him back to a deeper sleep. For a few minutes she thought she'd gotten her wish. Then the boy's eyes fluttered open, and he realized almost immediately that he'd been left alone.

"Daddy!" Panicky, Justin began to struggle to undo his seat belt.

Tina rapped on the window and called to him. If he got loose, there was no telling what he might do. She made a grab for the door handle and gave it a wrench. It didn't open!

"I'm here, Justin," she shouted. "I'm right here. It's okay. You're fine. Daddy will be right back."

The child began to sob. Tina pounded on the window with the flat of her hand, then ran around to try the doors on the opposite side. They were all locked. She knew she didn't dare leave the van long enough to fetch Zac. If Justin managed to undo his seat belt while she was gone, he might inadvertently slip the van into gear and cause an accident. If only his idiotic, overprotective father hadn't locked the blasted doors!

Close to panic herself, Tina shouted at the house. "Zac! Zac!" She needn't have worried that he might not hear her. In seconds he was charging across the lawn.

"What happened?"

"He woke up and…"

Zac reached for the door. "Why did you let him get so upset? I warned you…" He jerked the handle. Nothing happened! He whirled. "Why did you lock the door?"

"I didn't lock it. You did."

"No, I didn't."

"Well, *somebody* did," Tina countered. "Maybe you pushed the wrong button when you got out."

"No way." Zac's eyes widened. "Oh, no. He's loose." Fighting to appear calm, he called, "Hey, buddy. Here I am. Come open the door for Daddy."

The child was too overwrought to respond. He threw one foot up on the back of the front seat and was struggling to scramble over.

"We have to do something. We can't let him get to the driver's seat," Tina shouted.

"I know." Zac ran around to the other side of the van and dropped to his knees by the driver's door. He'd stashed an extra key under there for emergencies. What he hadn't counted on was the mud he found caked in hard ridges where the metal key holder should have been.

Scraping frantically with his fingernails, he called to Tina, "Get me something to break this off with!"

In the bedlam, Tina heard only part of his request. She quickly hefted a rock the size of a cantaloupe and whacked the front passenger window. Safety glass fragmented into a million tiny, harmless pieces the size of peas.

Zac came up off his knees with the box in his hand and a wild look on his face. "What the—?"

"You said to break it, so I did," she explained.

"Break the mud off my spare key—" he waved the muddy box "—not break the *window!*"

"Well, why didn't you say so?"

"I *did*." He swiftly unlocked the door on his side of the van and held out his arms. Justin was just landing in the front seat. Relieved, Zac grasped his small hand and helped him step down. "It's okay, son. I've got you."

The frightened boy wrapped his arms around his father's leg and held on as if it were a lifeline. His breath came in halting, shuddering sobs.

Waiting, Tina stood back and watched father and son try to regain their composure. Zac rested his hand on the boy's hair. When he tilted his head back and closed his eyes for a few seconds, Tina imagined him sending up a silent prayer of thanks. She'd already done the same. Breaking the window might be considered foolhardy by some people—but how was she to know Zac had a spare key? Given her assessment of the situation, she'd done the right thing. Anyway, Justin was safe. That was all that really mattered.

Acting on impulse, she approached the child, dropped to one knee beside him and began to gently stroke his back, while he continued to cling to Zac. "You're fine now, honey. Your daddy's right here. You know he'd never leave you."

To her surprise, Justin released his usual hold on his father's leg, threw himself at her, wrapped his little arms tightly around her neck and began to weep anew. Tina got down on both knees to hug him close.

"Oh, baby. Don't cry. Don't cry."

Tears of empathy filled her eyes and slid silently down her cheeks. This emotionally needy child had touched her as no other had. She kissed his hair, his wet cheeks, then cupped his face in her hands so he'd have to look at her when she reassured him.

"We love you, Justin. We'd never let anything bad happen to you."

As soon as she'd spoken she realized she'd made an inappropriate inference by combining her own compassion with that of Zac Frazier. Well, too bad. Knowing there was more than one person in the world who cared about him was critical to Justin's peace of mind. If his father didn't like it, tough.

She dried the child's tears with the hem of her skirt and made sure he'd stopped crying, before she gathered her courage and stood to confront Zac. "We need to discuss a few things, Mr. Frazier. In private."

To her surprise, he still seemed aggravated.

"Insurance will probably pay for the damage," Zac grumbled, scowling at his van. "What a mess. I wish you'd asked me instead of getting so carried away."

"You're worried about the mess from a broken window?" Exasperation filled Tina's voice. "Fine. I'll help you clean it up. But I don't give a hoot about your stupid window, okay? It's your son I'm worried about."

"You weren't so worried when you dropped broken *glass* all over him."

"All the new cars have safety glass. It's not sharp when it breaks. I knew it wouldn't hurt him."

"How about scare him to death," Zac countered. "He was already having a fit over waking up alone."

She wanted to scream, *So hug him. Show him some real affection,* but she held her tongue. Yelling at the man wasn't going change him, especially since he didn't seem to have a clue he was doing anything wrong. If he agreed to rent the property she'd shown him, however, she'd have lots of opportunities to observe his interaction with his son and offer a few subtle pointers on parenting. Unfortunately, with the Fraziers so close by, she wouldn't be able to escape from that duty, either. Even if she wanted to.

"So, are you going to take this house?" Tina asked, deliberately changing the subject. "You should commit yourself as soon as possible, you know. It won't stay empty for long." In her heart, she half hoped he'd say no, and relieve her of the God-given responsibility she was feeling.

"I suppose I will," Zac said flatly. "I haven't found any other place close to my job, and the rent is reasonable."

Well, that was that, Tina thought. She was stuck. "Okay. I'll let the landlord know. He can drop the rental agreement by your office, if you like."

"That'll be fine."

Tina held out her hand as if to shake on the deal, then quickly withdrew it when she recalled the way she'd reacted when they'd touched before. "Good night, then. I've done my good deed for the day, so

I guess I'll be going. Do you think you can find your way back to your motel by yourself?''

"Probably. Can I borrow a whisk broom and dust-pan before I go? I need to sweep up the broken glass.''

"And I said I'd help you, didn't I? I really am sorry. I was sure you said you wanted me to break the window.'' She flashed a wry smile.

"What I said was, give me something to break loose the dirt that was keeping me from getting to my spare key. I don't understand where all that hard mud came from. It hasn't rained since I've been here.''

"Probably from wasps. Mud daubers,'' Tina told him. "They make nests in everything, even motors. Thankfully, they're not as aggressive as the big, red, paper-wasps. Those can be nasty. If you see a nest with a bunch of exposed cells, kind of like honey-comb, *don't* put your hand into it.''

"I'll remember that. Thanks, neighbor.''

Neighbor? He soon would be, wouldn't he. Phooey. Well, like it or not, that was apparently what the Lord wanted, because the only available house in town was the one they were standing in front of.

How could she argue with providence? Clearly, God agreed that it would be much easier for her to help Justin if he lived close by. All she had to do was continue to keep his good-looking daddy at arm's length so she wouldn't be tempted to repeat past mistakes.

As Tina turned away to fetch the broom, her empty stomach growled. Combined with her guilt over not really wanting the Fraziers to become her neighbors, her hunger reminded her of Sunday's sermon about feeding a needy brother or sister. She didn't know how *needy* Zac and Justin might be, but it was long past her suppertime and she was starving to death. So why not invite them to eat with her?

Because it was a stupid idea, she argued. It was also a perfect opportunity to make them feel welcome and begin to educate Zac about children.

Hurrying back with the cleaning tools, she made her decision. "Why don't you two stay for supper? We can have a picnic in the backyard. I keep lots of hamburgers and hot dogs in the freezer, so I'm ready for any emergency."

Raising one eyebrow, Zac regarded her quizzically. "Is that local cuisine?"

"Not unless we wrap the whole sandwich in dough, dump it in a pan and deep fry it, too," Tina said with a light laugh. "Even some of the *pies* are fried around here."

"So I've heard. The thing that surprises me is how these people can live to be so old when they eat so much food that's supposed to be bad for you."

"Clean living— Was that a yes?"

"I think we could both use a break from restaurant food," Zac said, looking to his son for confirmation. "How about it, buddy? Want to eat at Miss Tina's tonight?"

"Yeah!"

Pleased, Zac nodded. "That makes it unanimous. We'll be over as soon as I get this mess..." His jaw dropped. Instead of clinging to him the way he usually did, Justin had raced back to Tina's side and immediately grabbed her hand.

"We'll wait for you," Tina said, careful to consider his feelings. He had been the boy's only refuge for a long time, and she didn't want him to think she was trying to take his place. "I'd rather cook outside in this kind of weather, and I'm probably going to need your help lighting the barbecue." Her grin widened. "I've heard that men are especially talented at getting cooking fires to burn properly."

"You heard right," Zac quipped. "We pass the secret down from generation to generation."

"I'd always suspected it was something like that. I hope you paid attention to your lessons. I don't want to use my stove unless I absolutely have to. Summer or winter."

"Spoken like a truly modern woman. Personally, I've found I like to cook. It's kind of a challenge."

"You're joking."

"No. Not at all." Bending over, he stuck his head and shoulders inside the van and continued to brush crystalline shards into the dustpan. "For instance, Justin and I love Mexican food. Around here, if you want a decent meal like that, you have to make it yourself."

"Boy, no kidding. I haven't had a good *chili relleno* since I left—" The color drained from her face.

Zac glanced up from his task. "Since you left where? Sorry. I didn't catch everything you just said."

Another close call! What was the matter with her? "Never mind. I was just rambling." All Tina wanted at that moment was to get away from him and restore her waning composure. "If you don't mind, I think Justin and I will go dig around in my freezer for something good to eat." She pushed aside her anxiety to smile down at the child.

"I'll come with you," Zac told her, straightening. "I've done about all I can with this broom. After dinner, maybe I can borrow your vacuum to finish the job."

"Sure. Always willing to be neighborly. Especially since the mess is my fault."

Feigning nonchalance, she led the way across the adjoining lawns to her house. On the outside she was calm. Inside, her thoughts whirled madly. What had lowered her defenses and loosened her tongue? It had been over a year since she'd moved to Serenity and gone to work for Mavis, yet until recently she'd never mentioned anything that might accidentally lead someone to discover her secret shame. Now, all of a sudden, she was turning into a regular fountain of information. Why in the world was that happening?

Tina felt her pulse pound in her temples. When

she'd first come to Serenity, she'd purposely adopted a new last name, a simple, traditional persona; kept to herself and had never so much as jaywalked, for fear of exposure. Her current life was an open book: Tina Braddock, volume two.

It was volume *one* she didn't want anyone to know about.

Justin lost interest in the adults as soon as he met Zorro, Tina's eccentric black-and-white cat. Its body was too long in proportion to its legs, it had the distinctive yowl of a Siamese and its favorite game was hide-and-seek. The game was in full swing on and around the back porch by the time Zac had the barbecue fire going.

"That animal is crazy." Scowling, he watched the outlandish cat hide behind the crossed legs of a picnic table and pounce on Justin's shoes as soon as the boy got close enough. "You're sure he's not dangerous?"

"Positive. I've even taken him to the preschool with me to show the children. He's never laid a paw on any of them."

"How about his claws?"

"He doesn't have any front ones." Tina took note of Zac's look of disapproval. "I didn't have his claws removed, if that's what you're thinking. It had already been done when I adopted him."

"You didn't get him as a kitten?" Listening, he leaned down to blow more air on the fire.

"No. He used to belong to one of the Whitaker sisters. When they sold their property they were desperate to find homes for Miss Prudence's cats, so I said I'd take one."

Zac arched an eyebrow as he watched the cat-versus-boy game progressing. "You picked *him?*"

"Not exactly," Tina said. "Zorro was the only one they had left by the time I got there. I took him because I felt sorry for him. If I'd known what a character he was, I'd have chosen him, anyway. They told me he got his name because he always zigzagged when he ran." She placed a finger in front of her lips. "Look. He's hiding under the wicker chair. See his tail twitching out the back? Watch what he does when I sit down there."

Justin raced by. Zac reached out to slow his progress. "Miss Tina wants us to watch something. Over there—" He crouched down beside the boy and pointed.

Still barefoot, Tina sauntered up to the chair, carefully sat down and began to swing her feet. In seconds the mischievous feline launched his attack. Wrapping his forelegs around her ankle, he pretended to bite it while his hind feet raked at her defenseless foot. If Zac hadn't seen her giggling, he'd have been certain she was being hurt.

She bent over and began to tickle the cat's tummy. It leaped to its feet and sprinted off in a blur of black and white, followed by the little boy.

"Zorro can dish it out but he can't take it," Tina

remarked, grinning. "He loves to play that game. Especially when I act like I don't know he's there. I think he's a frustrated predator. I suppose all indoor cats are."

"Indoor? Uh-oh. You should have said something when Justin let him out. I never thought about it being a problem, or I'd have stopped him."

"It's fine as long as I'm here," Tina assured him. "Without his front claws, Zorro would be helpless if he had to defend himself, though. He acts ferocious but he's really a marshmallow." Her smile broadened. "Hey! That reminds me. I think I have a bag of marshmallows in the pantry. Want to roast them for dessert?"

Justin's loud "Yeah!" startled the cat and sent him on another wild lap over and under the raised wooden porch. On the final pass he disappeared into the shadowy recesses beneath the steps.

"Speaking as a guidance counselor," Zac gibed, "it's my professional opinion that your cat is severely disturbed."

"Oh? What treatment would you recommend? Do you want to sit down with him and ask him about his early years?"

"If he were a person, that's exactly what I'd do. You'd be amazed at the stories I've heard since I got my degree and started working with teens. It's appalling."

Turning away, Tina busied herself smoothing a fresh plastic cloth over the picnic table. *Appalling* was only the beginning. Given her experience with her younger brother, Craig, she could have added *unbelievable,* and *terrifying,* and *life-shattering.* Especially life-shattering.

The only good thing to come out of the situation with Craig was his eventual rehabilitation. Seeing him settled down with a wife, son and new baby almost made it all worthwhile. Almost.

If she had it to do over again, however, Tina knew she'd find some other way to help him. And she'd never tell a lie. Not one. Not even if her honesty meant her unmanageable sibling might have to suffer.

Justin ran out of steam right after they ate. Five minutes of whining were followed by blissful silence, when he curled up in the big wicker chair and dozed off.

"I've always preferred dogs, myself," Zac said, "but I think I may need to borrow your crazy cat from time to time. My son hasn't gone to sleep that easily for longer than I can remember."

"You could always get him a puppy, you know. Your new yard is already fenced to keep it home." Tina scanned the yard and porch. "Poor Zorro. I'll bet he's crawled off for a catnap. Chances are, he's exhausted, too."

"It wore me out just watching them play."

"I know what you mean. Me, too." She stood and began to gather up the dishes, surprised when Zac picked up his plate and rose to help her. She waved him off. "I can do this. Sit down. You're my guest."

"I'd rather help."

He sounded so sincere, she gave in. "Okay. Make a stack on the end of the kitchen counter, just inside the door. That way you'll be in sight if Justin stirs."

Complying, Zac watched her carry the uneaten food past him and put it in the refrigerator. He sighed and spoke softly. "I'm at my wits' end with that kid. I'd hoped that a change of scenery would stop his panic attacks."

"Instead of a dog, maybe he needs more family in his life so he doesn't concentrate solely on you. Aren't there any female relatives you could ask for help?"

"Oh, sure," he said cynically. "Kim—my wife— came from a big family. All three of her sisters dote on Justin."

"Well, then...?"

"No way." Zac was shaking his head. "They hate me. If I give them the chance to fill Justin's head with their unfair opinions, he might wind up hating me, too. At the very least, he'd be more confused than he already is."

Tina couldn't imagine anyone disliking a man like Zac. Even though he was clumsy at expressing affection, he clearly loved his son. Pensive, she led the way back outside and started to fold up the plastic tablecloth. "You really believe they'd do that?"

"In a heartbeat." His voice deepened. "They blame me for Kim's death."

Hoping he'd explain further, Tina hugged the folded cloth to her chest and waited quietly. She knew better than to question him on such a touchy subject, even though her curiosity was aroused. Once they officially became neighbors, perhaps he'd volunteer more information. If not, she'd just have to respect his privacy.

Finally, she broke down and asked, "What about your side of the family? Brothers? Sisters?"

Zac snorted with derision. "I was an only child. My parents live in a retirement community down in Florida. Justin and I detoured to visit them on our way here. Talk about a disaster. All my mother did when he got upset was wring her hands and cry right along with him." A wry smile lifted one corner of Zac's mouth. "It was quite a chorus. You should have seen the look on my dad's face."

"I'll bet."

Stuffing his hands into his pockets he began, "I've been thinking. Maybe..."

Tina intuitively finished his sentence. "You thought maybe I'd volunteer?"

"I suppose that's too much to ask."

"No. Not at all."

Tina had to struggle to keep from laughing at the smooth way the Lord had handled a potentially awkward situation. While she'd been needlessly fretting about how she was going to worm her way into the little boy's life without having her innocent motives misunderstood, God was setting the whole thing up. What a kick. Everything was turning out *exactly* as she'd planned, yet Zac Frazier thought the whole idea was his!

Chapter Four

little boy, she wondered what prevented unreson
maintaining. She'd was staring the what, thing up
what middle I wounds't gas that's our garld...
she drinked of I... Zac her lorching in the whole
open was list.

Chapter Four

Zac had offered to paint the interior of the house as soon as it was vacant because he wanted to expedite his tenancy. However, he'd had no idea how hard the job would be, especially with Justin underfoot every second.

By the time he'd finished putting one coat of paint on the master bedroom, there were already tiny sneaker prints of the same pale beige color up and down the hall.

Tina found the little boy sitting on the steps of his new front porch, barefoot. She joined him. "Hi, honey."

Justin cast her a forlorn look.

"Uh-oh," she said, smiling tenderly. "What's wrong?"

"Daddy's mad at me."

Tina drew up her knees and hugged them. "Are you sure?"

"Uh-huh. He hollered at me."

"My, that sounds serious. Why do you suppose he got so upset?"

"'Cause of that dumb old paint."

"What did the paint do?"

"It stuck to my shoes and got itself all over the rug."

"That *was* bad," she said, working hard to sound serious when what she wanted to do was laugh out loud at his childish logic. "Is that why you're sitting on the porch?"

The boy nodded. "Daddy took my shoes off and told me to stay right here." His voice quieted. "Dumb old paint."

"I'm pretty good with a brush. Do you suppose your daddy would like me to help him?" she asked, getting to her feet and smoothing her shorts as she spoke. "Maybe I should go see."

"Okay," Justin said with a sage expression, "'cept he might yell at you, too."

Tina slipped off her sandals by the front door. "I hope not, but just in case, I'll leave my shoes out here. That way I'll feel it if I accidentally step in any spilled paint, and I won't track it all over the place."

Leaving the unhappy child to mull over her common sense approach, she let herself in and called, "Yoo-hoo. Anybody home?"

"In here. Down the hall," he answered gruffly. "Watch your step. The carpet's wet."

She edged past the obviously damp portions and paused at the bedroom door. Zac had carefully covered the carpeting in that room with plastic sheeting, taped down at the edges. It was easy to see that Justin had tracked through every drop of paint he could find on the plastic, then headed for the hallway. His footprints stopped where the wet carpeting began.

Tina giggled. "I see your son was helping you paint this morning."

"Helping me lose my mind, you mean." He made a sour face. "It's not funny."

"Oh, I don't know. It proves what I've always heard. You catch insanity from your children." Taking in the room and its occupant, she shook her head and grinned. Zac had paint smeared on his shorts and tank top, plus splatters on nearly every inch of exposed skin. "Are you trying to paint the walls or decorate yourself?"

He was obviously in no mood for her sarcasm. One eyebrow arched as he stared back at her. "What does it look like?"

"Truthfully? It looks like you aren't sure. You've got paint in your hair and beige freckles all over your face and arms, among other things."

"That's probably gray you see in my hair, thanks to Justin," Zac countered. "So far, I've spent more time cleaning up after that kid than I have slinging paint at these four walls."

"So *that's* your problem," Tina gibed. "Well, no wonder. You're supposed to *roll* it on, not sling it."

"I'm glad *somebody* is amused."

"I certainly am." Laughing lightly, she waited for his expression to soften. It finally did. "That's better. Now, tell me. Would you rather I took Justin home with me to get him out of your rapidly graying hair, or pitched in and helped you paint this place?"

"I don't suppose there's any way you can do both, is there?"

"I'm good, but I'm not *that* good. Tell you what. I'll go change into some old clothes and bring Zorro back with me when I come. That way you'll have a painting partner and Justin will have something to occupy him while we finish up in here. How's that sound?"

"Like heaven," Zac said with a sigh. "I'm not real good at painting houses."

"Noooo," she mocked. "Do tell."

One corner of his mouth twitched in a wry smile, and he hefted the paint roller by its handle, as if testing it for weight and balance. "You're lucky you already volunteered to help me, Miss Tina. If you hadn't, I might be tempted to do something rash."

She quickly ducked around the doorjamb and peeked out from behind it, eyes sparkling with mischief. "You do, and I'll turn *you* purple the way you threatened to do to poor, innocent little Tommy."

"I'd like to see you try," Zac shot back.

Tina laughed and shook her head. "Oh, no, you wouldn't. Trust me. You'd lose."

"Oh, yeah?"

"Yeah. But right now, I think we'd better concentrate on getting your house painted. Are you planning on doing the other bedrooms, too?"

"That's what the landlord said he wants, and he bought the paint, so I guess the answer is yes. Since I was stupid enough to offer in the first place, I'm stuck doing things his way."

"Okay. Go tape the plastic down in the other rooms and get them ready. I'll be back in a jiffy."

Zac snorted derisively. "Do you always jump in with both feet and start giving orders?"

"Only when it's obvious I'm dealing with somebody whose expertise is sorely lacking in an area where I shine. You have a choice. You can either listen to my good advice or struggle through this project the hard way. Alone."

"Is that a threat or a promise?" he asked.

"Both." Wheeling, she flounced off down the hall.

Zac watched his charming neighbor go, then stood motionless for a few moments more after she was out of sight. He didn't realize how much her presence had distracted him until he looked down at the roller in his hand. Paint had pooled in the lowest point of the cylinder and was falling in a thin stream, making squiggle lines all over the tops of his running shoes.

* * *

Tina wasted no time returning, as promised. She found Zac crawling around on his hands and knees, securing the protective plastic sheet in the smaller bedroom.

"You don't need to mask those baseboards," she told him, pausing in the doorway. "I have a very steady hand."

"I'm glad one of us does." He looked up. "Did you check on Justin when you went outside?"

Tina nodded. "He's fine. He and Zorro are playing cat-and-mouse. Justin's the mouse."

"That's typecasting, for sure. The kid loves cheese."

"And Zorro's already a cat, so he's a natural, too," Tina added, playing along. "Did you finish the master bedroom, or do I need to go back and touch it up for you?"

"It's done. At least, I think it is. I had to stop to scrub footprints off the carpeting in the hall, and by the time I got back the fresh paint was so dry it was hard to tell where I'd left off. You might want to see if I missed any spots."

"Okay. Back in a flash."

Zac straightened and rubbed the back of his neck with one hand. That woman was a wonder. Nothing seemed to faze her. Didn't she ever get grumpy? One thing was for sure, she always managed to look good, no matter how she was dressed. When she'd first come over she'd been wearing a turquoise shirt and shorts that had set off the greenish tint of her eyes.

This time, although she'd donned tattered denim shorts and tied the tails of an old blouse at her waist, she still looked appealing.

Face it, Frazier, he told himself. *Like it or not, you have a pretty neighbor.*

Which makes no difference to me at all, he added quickly, defensively. *The only thing I care about is raising my son the way Kim would have wanted.*

Guilt instantly filled his heart. If he intended to instill the right values and set the right kind of example, he'd better start taking Justin to Sunday School again. That kind of thing had mattered to Kim. It mattered to him, too. Once, he and his late wife had led a youth ministry that had been a miraculous success, due in part to his contacts with teens through his counseling job. He could do that again. He *should* do it again.

Tina appeared in the doorway with the roller, pan and one of the partially used gallons of paint, bringing an end to his solitary contemplation.

"I found a couple of streaks in the other room and painted over them," she said. "Otherwise, you did a fine job."

"Thanks." Zac got to his feet. "Okay. You're the boss. Tell me what to do now. I'm all yours." The rosy blush rising to her cheeks made him add, "Figuratively speaking, of course."

"Of course." Embarrassed, she averted her gaze and busied herself with the painting supplies as she spoke. "I noticed that all the paint was the same color. That's good. It means we won't have to wash the brushes and roller between rooms. And I brought some plastic wrap from my kitchen, in case you don't have any, so we can cover the tray whenever we take a break. That way, the extra paint won't dry in the pan or on the roller and be wasted.''

''Sounds like you have it all figured out.''

She chanced a peek up at him. ''All but the ladder part. As you may have noticed, I'm a little short on one end. And I get dizzy on ladders, so I'd prefer you take charge of the ceilings and the tops of the walls.''

''Oh, I don't know,'' Zac drawled. ''Your legs must be the right length, they...''

''They reach all the way to the ground. Yeah, yeah. I've heard that my whole life.''

''Sorry. Just trying to be friendly.''

''I know. Guess I'm overly sensitive about my height.''

''Lack of height, you mean,'' Zac offered with a lopsided smile. ''I suppose that's one reason you relate to little kids so well. You're practically on their level.''

''Mister,'' Tina retorted, ''I'm on their level in more ways than just my size. I even think their lame jokes are funny.'' She stirred the paint remaining in the can, then poured more into the roller pan. ''Yesterday, Tommy asked me why the chicken crossed the road.''

''To get to the other side?''

"Humph. That's what I guessed, too. Tommy said, nope, it crossed the road because the Colonel was after it! Broke me up."

"Sounds like that kid eats out a lot. Which reminds me," Zac said without considering the possible ramifications, "I owe you a dinner."

"Thought you'd never ask."

"Whoa." He shook his head, incredulous. "I wasn't exactly asking. I was merely making an observation. There's nothing to eat in my kitchen. Not even a table to sit at. And by the time we finish this job, I don't think either of us will be in any shape to go out to eat, so..."

"So, order a pizza delivered, and we'll eat it on the porch. I'm not fussy." The consternation on his face struck her as funny. "Don't look so scared. I'm not making a pass at you. It's local custom. We Southerners are always feeding each other. Take my church, for instance. If we didn't have a dinner on the ground once in a while after the morning service, we wouldn't think we were in the right place."

"Dinner on the *what?*"

Tina watched him stand the stepladder near the corner and wiggle it to make sure it was safe to climb. "On the ground. It's one of those old sayings we were talking about, before. Back in horse-and-buggy days, lots of folks traveled a long way to worship. After the morning service, they used to spread out blankets on the ground and share food, then fellowship together all afternoon before starting for home.''

She chuckled at his cautious expression. ''Hey, don't worry. We eat at tables, now. And we don't do it every Sunday. Just occasionally. Matter of fact, there's one planned for this weekend.''

''Too bad it's not Sunday till tomorrow, then,'' Zac said. ''I could use some good home cooking.''

Tina handed him the roller and pan, steadying the ladder while he climbed it and started painting the ceiling. ''I thought you said you liked to cook.''

''I used to. I haven't felt much like doing it lately.''

Pausing to decide if she should keep still and let him reveal more details at his own speed, or question him about his past, Tina suddenly realized he'd hinted he might like to come to her church. She took that as a very good sign. ''You know, if you bring a covered dish to the church dinner, you'll be the hit of the afternoon. What were some of your favorite recipes?''

''I liked to experiment with ethnic food. Mexican, Chinese, stuff like that.'' He heard her melodic laugh below him and leaned over to peer down at her. ''What?''

''Nothing. Just that I tried to get a few of my local friends to taste my homemade salsa, and they looked at me like I was crazy. Finally, I settled on a couple of recipes everybody liked, and now I take the same dishes to church suppers virtually every time.''

"Maybe I should try—"

There was a howl from the direction of the front porch. Zac froze, listening. "What the...?"

Tina was already headed for the door at a trot. "Sounds like Zorro's in trouble. I'll go see what's wrong."

"Not without me, you won't," he said. Jumping down and dashing after her, he shouted, "Justin! You okay?"

Tina reached the front door a heartbeat ahead of Zac and straight-armed the screen. It swung all the way open and smacked against the house with a loud, metallic *bang*.

It didn't take a half-second for her to assess the problem. Justin was perched astride the wooden porch railing, trying to hold on to her struggling cat, while a rambunctious, half-grown, yellowish dog barked beneath them.

"How did *that* get in the yard?" Zac shouted.

"Probably jumped the fence. It's big enough."

Zac pushed past her and reached for his son, ordering the boy, "Let go of the cat."

Justin clung to the frightened Zorro for all he was worth. "No! No!"

"Here. I'll take him," Tina said.

Before she could act, however, Zac had grabbed Justin around the waist and pulled him close, leaving her poor pet pinned between them. Thank goodness the cat had been declawed or he'd have torn up father and son like a miniature buzz saw.

Zorro continued to yowl unmercifully. The stray dog apparently thought everybody had come outside to play, because he got even more excited and began leaping awkwardly into the air next to Zac, thoroughly discombobulating the trapped cat.

"Give me my kitty!" Tina shouted over the din.

Zac had his hands full. "Get that dog out of here, first."

She had to admit, the man had a point. Without the added agitation, Zorro would be a lot easier to handle. The trouble was, the adolescent canine wasn't cooperating. Every time she reached for him, he ducked away. Finally, she lunged with her whole body and managed to drape her torso over his back long enough to get both arms around his neck and bring him to a halt. Sort of.

"*Now* what do I do?" she asked, panting.

"Hang on!" Zac ordered. "I'm putting these two in the house where they'll be safe."

Tina didn't have the time or the inclination to question his decision. She was having enough trouble keeping hold of the dog. Its ears and feet were enormous. The rest of it didn't look fully developed but clearly promised to be gargantuan once it matured. Fortunately, it had an amiable temperament. Instead of trying to bite Tina, it was licking her face and wiggling all over with delight.

She wasn't nearly that happy about their close association. The reappearance of Zac looming over her would have been a more welcome sight if he hadn't been just standing there. Dodging the dog's wet tongue, she peered up at him.

"It's about time. Get this moose away from me!"

"You all right?"

"I will be when you *help* me." She suspected he was delaying because he was so amused by her predicament.

"Right. Got him," Zac finally said. "You can let go now."

Breathless, she fell back into a spraddle-legged position on the porch floor. Zac had grabbed the dog around its rib cage, the way she'd first tried to do, and lifted it off the ground, its back against his chest. Held in that position, the animal stiffened, its lanky legs pointed straight out as if they had each miraculously acquired splints. Only the dog's tail continued to move. It was hanging down between Zac's legs and wagging slightly.

"He's almost as tall as you are," Tina marveled. "Must be part Great Dane."

"No kidding. Where does he belong?"

"Beats me. Maybe he'll go home if you put him outside the fence."

"I sure hope so." Zac cautiously started down the porch steps. "I'd hate to have to go through all this again."

Exhausted from her wrestling match with the friendly pup, Tina took a deep, settling breath. "Boy, you and me, both."

She saw Zac stop at the gate, but he couldn't reach

the latch to open it because of the dog's stiff-legged posture.

"Want some help?" she called, her voice overly sweet.

"Oh, no," he replied, puffing and straining. "I'll just…hoist him up…over my head…and lower him gently on the other side of this five-foot-high fence." His voice rose. "Of *course*, I want some help!"

"Well, you don't have to get huffy." Stifling her giggles, Tina scrambled to her feet and hurried to join him. "That really is a sweet dog," she said, pausing to ruffle its satiny ears with one hand while she unlatched the gate with the other. "He could have had us all for lunch, yet he never once growled, not even when I fell all over him and grabbed him."

"Before you get too softhearted, I suggest you keep in mind that it was your *cat* he wanted to eat for lunch, not people."

"That's certainly what poor Zorro thought. What a funny picture we must have made, with Justin trying to keep him safe from this dog and you and me wrestling both animals."

"No kidding. I'm glad nobody was videotaping us." Zac lowered the dog gently to the ground, hind feet first, intending to steady him before letting him go.

Instead of standing up or running away, however, the big dog collapsed in a heap at his feet and rolled on its back in submission, its wide, pink tongue lolling out the side of its mouth.

"I think you win, Zac. Looks like he's accepted you as his boss."

Tina bent down to gently scratch the dog's stomach, and it moved one of its hind legs in unison with her ministrations, as if it were doing the scratching, instead. "Look. He's giving us the chance to conquer him and hoping for kindness, just like a weaker animal would do in the wild."

Zac wiped perspiration off his brow with the back of his hand and leaned against the gatepost. "Goody. Now I get to be his idol. Lucky me."

"Well, that's better than being his enemy, considering his size. When I first saw him, I thought he might be a yellow Lab, but he's way too big for that. If he grows into those feet, he'll be a monster. He'd better like us. We have to live in this neighborhood, too, you know."

Straightening and backing through the gate so she could close it while leaving their canine nemesis shut out, she noticed that Zac was frowning down at her. "What's wrong?"

He folded his arms across his broad chest. "Oh, nothing much. It just occurred to me that since you live around here you should know who he belongs to, unless he's a stray. He is kind of hard to overlook."

"He wasn't wearing any collar," Tina added soberly. "That's why I had to grab him like I was trying to throw a steer at a rodeo."

"He's not quite *that* big."

"Give him a month or two. He'll grow."

"Yeah. I hate to just leave him out here and hope he'll go home, but I don't know what else to do with him." Zac glanced toward the house. "Well, I suppose we'd better get back to our painting or we'll still be at it tonight."

"Painting!" Tina gasped. "Oh, no." Eyes wide, she stared up at her companion. "We left a kid and a scared cat loose inside your house with all that paint!"

Chapter Five

It wasn't hard to trace Zorro's path. Once he'd visited the room where Zac had left the open roller pan, his tracks were easy to follow. The more steps he took, however, the more his paw prints faded. Justin's bare footprints were beside the cat's for the last part of its journey. Both sets of tracks disappeared in the kitchen.

Zac raked his fingers through his hair and shook his head. "I don't believe this."

"I wonder where they went," Tina said with a chuckle.

"Out the back door, I hope," Zac mumbled, rapidly crossing to a window that looked out on the fenced backyard, to satisfy himself that his son was safe. "They're there."

"That's one thing to be thankful for. Got a mop?"

Leaning to one side, she was sighting along the shiny floor, looking for dull spots of smeared paint.

"No. But I'll buy one. I'm going to have to give up painting for the day and go rent a rug shampoo machine at the closest supermarket, anyway. I'll get a mop, too, if they have one. Can you look after Justin while I'm gone?"

"Sure. I'll take him home with me."

"*And* the cat."

Tina tried to smother a burst of giggles and failed. "And the cat," she agreed. "I wouldn't have brought him over here to keep Justin company if I'd had any idea he'd start so much trouble."

Zac was washing paint spots off his hands and forearms at the kitchen sink. "Glad to hear it was spontaneous. I'd hate to think you got up this morning already determined to ruin my day."

"Naw," Tina said with a teasing grin. "I only do that to my enemies."

"You have enemies? Here in Serenity? I'm amazed."

It was the fading of her bright smile, rather than anything she said in return, that showed him he'd touched a nerve.

Lowering her gaze, she said flatly, "No. I have no enemies. Not anymore."

All the way to the supermarket and all the way home, Zac thought about how forlorn Tina had looked when their innocent banter had gotten too close to whatever painful truth she felt the need to hide.

What she did, said or felt was none of his business, he told himself firmly. The woman had already proved she was a walking disaster waiting to happen. If he let himself get too close to her, he was liable to find out his "Miss Tina" problems had only just begun.

Kim would have liked her, he decided. Would have befriended her. And eventually probably would have become her confidant the way she had with some of the troubled teenage girls in their former youth group. How old was Tina Braddock, anyway? It was hard to tell when she acted so unrestrained. Not that her company manners weren't first-rate. She just struck him as more of a kid at heart than most other adults did—which wasn't a bad trait to have in view of her job at the day care center.

He pulled his van into his driveway and got out to unload the carpet-cleaning machine. All seemed quiet in the rural neighborhood. That was probably due, in part at least, to the uncomfortably high afternoon temperature.

Toting his rental and the special soap to fill it, Zac let himself in the back door. An unbelievable sight stopped him in his tracks. His four-year-old son was down on his hands and knees, scrubbing the floor with a stiff brush, while Tina stood over him and pointed out spots he'd missed!

It was all Zac could do to keep from cursing.

"What do you think you're doing?" he bellowed, staring at Tina.

"Cleaning up after ourselves," she replied calmly. "We make the mess, we clean it up." Her steady gaze dared him to contradict her.

"Four-year-olds are *not* responsible for scrubbing floors."

"They are if they dirty them through carelessness when they know better." Hands on her hips, she faced Zac squarely. "Or would you like to wait until he's oh, say, fifteen or sixteen, and *then* try to convince him that there are consequences to everything he does, good or bad?"

"That's not the point."

"That is *exactly* the point," Tina insisted.

Zac glanced at his son's upturned face and saw tears glistening in his eyes. His stance softened. "I'm sorry I got upset, buddy. I'm not mad at you. I was just surprised, that's all."

"We...we got it all clean in here," the boy said with a quaver in his voice. "Miss Tina helped. She did Zorro's footprints, 'cause he's her cat—and I did mine."

"I see." Zac felt like a heel. "Then, I guess I owe Miss Tina an apology."

"Apology accepted," she said with a wry grimace. "I apologize, too, for not asking you if it was all right for me to discipline your child in your absence. I get so used to doing it at work, I tend to forget I'm not responsible for every kid I meet."

"Aren't you? In a way, I think we're all responsible," Zac told her. "Or, at least, we should be."

Tina was in awe. "You mean that?"

"Every word. Which is one of the reasons I've decided to start going to church, again. Justin needs it. And maybe I do, too. Who knows? I might even be led to help with another youth group, the way I used to. I certainly have enough practical experience and the right credentials to qualify for the job." He'd been unwinding the power cord to the shampooer as he spoke, and handed the plug to Tina when she approached.

"Is that what you eventually want to do?" she asked softly. "Be a church youth director?"

"Something like that, Lord willing. It was an old dream I'd pretty much given up on. I'm beginning to believe I had to come to Serenity to rediscover what's really important."

Rather than dash his hopes, at least regarding the rules of the church she belonged to, Tina kept silent. The deacons had already rejected several unmarried applicants for the part-time job of youth pastor. They'd insisted that a man had to be settled, with a well-rounded family of his own, before he was suited to handling other people's children.

Still, though he was single, Zac *was* a father and a widower rather than a divorced man, so perhaps he would qualify. If not, there were plenty of local women who would be eager to volunteer to complete his family portrait by becoming his wife.

Tina pictured the female assault that would ensue as soon as the eligible women in town found out about his marital status. He'd be up to his eyebrows in casseroles and homemade cakes before he knew what hit him. Living practically next door, she'd be lucky if she wasn't trampled in the stampede.

"Well, at least I don't have to worry about competing," Tina muttered to herself.

"Worry?" Zac asked. "I didn't hear all that. Were you worried about the carpeting?"

"Right." Tina took it as a gift from the Lord that her companion had thought she'd said "carpeting" instead of "competing." "I scrubbed the hallway to get up the worst of Zorro's tracks. I left the rug really wet on purpose, so I think everything else will come out okay." She put on a happy face. "So, shall I stay and help you, or do you want me to take the kids home with me?"

"Kids? Plural?"

"Justin and Zorro. Our mischievous children," she explained, smiling. The smile he gave her in return had to be warm enough to melt a glacier.

"Why don't you run on home. I should have this job done in about an hour, especially if I don't have to keep one eye on my son."

"Or the other eye on my cat. When you came in just now, did you happen to see the big dog lurking outside?"

"Come to think if it, no, I didn't. Maybe he's gone back where he came from."

"Then, things are looking up," Tina said, starting for the door. "If you want, you can have the pizza delivered to my house, since I'm the one with a table and chairs. Unless you have your heart set on eating out on the porch, now that the dog's gone."

Zac had forgotten all about his half-baked dinner invitation. He was tired, in desperate need of a shower and feeling a lot less cordial than normal. However, he supposed it was best to get it over with. Cancelling his social obligations to Tina by sharing a casual meal like pizza seemed to offer a painless solution.

"You order it and I'll pay for it," Zac said. "My treat. Order plenty. And get some soda pop, too. I'm going to let Justin live it up tonight and drink that instead of having milk with his meal."

"Wow. Wild, aren't you?" she quipped.

"I've had my moments, especially when I was younger. Admitting my own mistakes helps me relate to the kids I work with. Now, go on. I have to get busy before the swamp you left in the hall dries."

Tina was thankful he'd turned away and started fiddling with the shampooer. *Mistakes?* she thought. *Oh, mister, you have no idea how bad some people's mistakes can be. Like mine, for instance.* If anyone in Serenity ever found out, they'd probably run her out of town on a rail.

She'd decided long ago not to let herself get too close to other people or make friends who might ask questions about her past. Remaining aloof wasn't easy, but it was necessary. And as long as she had other people's children to love and care for, the self-enforced solitude was bearable.

Above all, she must *never* allow herself to fall in love, she added, gritting her teeth. It would be the most unfair thing she could do to anyone, including herself. She'd found out the hard way that no decent man would want her, least of all a man in the public eye.

Least of all, a man with plans like Zac Frazier's.

Zac was worn out by the time he finished the carpet. He cut across the neighbors' lawns and headed for Tina's back door rather than take the chance of tracking dirt into her living room.

He didn't see anyone in the kitchen when he peered through the screen, so he called out, "Hi. Anybody home?"

Whooping, Justin came on the run to let him in. "Daddy!"

"Hi, buddy. Have you been good?"

Tina answered for him as she walked into the kitchen carrying two red-and-white pizza boxes. "He's been wonderful. And your timing is perfect. The food just arrived. I had plenty of sodas in the fridge so I didn't bother to order more."

"Smells great. How much do I owe you?" Zac pulled out his wallet.

She waved him off. "Nothing. I took care of it."

"Oh, no, you don't," he insisted. "Either you let me pay, or Justin and I are out of here."

"Aw, Da-a-a-ad," the boy whined.

"Okay, okay." The printed bill was taped to the top box. Tina pulled it loose and passed it to him. "Sorry. It looks like we could have had a fancy dinner at Linden's for less money."

"Linden's?"

"It's a big buffet over in East Serenity. Practically everybody goes there after church. It's an all-you-can-eat place."

Laying the money on the kitchen counter, then taking a seat at her table, Zac helped Justin into the chair beside him and checked the boy's hands to make sure they were reasonably clean. "I thought you said there was a potluck coming up at your church?"

"This Sunday there is. We don't do it all the time, though." As soon as she'd provided their drinks, Tina sat down across from her guests and began to dish up the pizza. She smiled as she handed a plate to Zac. "So, what were you planning to bring?"

One dark eyebrow arched. "A bag of potato chips?"

"Well..."

"A *big* bag?"

"That'll do if you want to pretend you're a helpless bachelor with a poor, starving child to feed."

Justin laughed. So did his father.

"It will also mean that every single lady for fifty

miles in any direction will be showing up at your door, trying to win you over with her cooking.''

''Are you serious?''

''Count on it,'' Tina said. ''That's why we don't have many bachelors left around here. At least, not ones with teeth.''

Zac sounded as if he was going to strangle. He covered his mouth with his napkin till he got better control of himself. ''I'm so glad you told me that.''

''Just trying to warn you.''

''Maybe I should build a brick wall around my house and dig myself a moat.''

''Wouldn't help,'' she countered. ''The ladies I know would get past a little obstacle like a moat, even if it was full of alligators.''

Zac froze, a wedge of pizza halfway to his mouth. ''You don't really have alligators in this part of Arkansas, do you?'' He cast a sidelong glance at his young son. ''If I thought...''

''Nope. Just enough ticks, chiggers and mosquitoes to make life miserable in the summer and enough ice on the roads to make it interesting for a few days each winter. Other than that, this is a pretty nice place to live.''

''I'll buy some bug repellent the next time I go to the store. Anything else you think I need?''

''Not unless they've started selling a product you can spray on to keep the women away,'' she teased.

The man was staring at her in disbelief, acting as if he didn't know how attractive he really was.

Maybe he didn't. But he was sure going to find out. He really was the best-looking, most appealing guy in Serenity—or in all of Fulton County, for that matter—and his son was a charmer, too.

Truth to tell, if she hadn't considered herself unacceptable wife material for anyone, let alone Zac Frazier, she might have jumped in line with a casserole of her own and given the other single women a run for their money.

Justin had asked to be excused from the table and had promptly fallen asleep in an overstuffed chair in Tina's living room. She was combining the leftover pizza into one box, when Zac returned to the kitchen to report why the boy was suddenly so quiet.

"I noticed he could barely keep his eyes open." Tina gestured with the open box. "Here. Sure I can't talk you into one more slice?"

"Uh-uh. I ate too much already." Rejoining her at the table, Zac leaned back in his chair and lazily studied the kitchen. "You know, this is a cute little house. I like the way you've fixed it up."

"Thanks. It's exactly the same as the one you're renting, except the floor plan is reversed."

"You're kidding! This place feels a lot more homey."

"Must be because of the frilly curtains on the window over the sink," she alibied, hoping he'd drop the subject before she began to blush.

"I don't know." He laced his fingers behind his

head in a classic pose of relaxation. "I suppose I could try that at my place and see if it helps. You've got little statues and things sitting all over, too. And houseplants. I never was any good at keeping those alive. I got so I felt guilty for dooming the poor things by buying them in the first place."

"Then, why did you?"

Zac sighed. "Because Kim had always liked them so much. Keeping the house full of greenery made it seem more like she was still around."

"I'm sorry. I shouldn't have asked."

"It's okay. As long as Justin's not here to listen to us, I don't mind talking about her."

Tina began to frown. "You don't talk to him about his mother? Why not?"

"It brings back the trauma."

"How do you know?"

"Because I've seen how he acts when I mention Kim. He gets all tense and red-faced, then he starts to cry."

"Every time?"

"Every time. I took him to several doctors, but they couldn't even get him to talk to them, let alone to explain what was bothering him."

"His mother died. That's what was bothering him."

"I mean, specifically," Zac said soberly.

"Isn't he more likely to tell *you* something like that than he is to confide in a stranger?"

"Not necessarily. I told you, I don't relate well to small children. Not even Justin."

"Maybe that's because you think of the little ones as being more different than they really are. If he were a sad teenager, what would you do? How would you approach him?"

Tina saw his relaxed posture stiffen, his jaw muscles tense.

"I'd do the same thing I already did," Zac said flatly. "Find my son a capable, professional counselor."

"Which is exactly what *you* are. Plus, you love him. I know you do. Is there some good reason why you don't step into that role yourself?"

Zac got to his feet and stood facing her, pausing only long enough to say "Yes. I'm the one who's responsible for his mother's death, and he knows it. He saw it happen with his own eyes."

Tina was so overburdened by her turbulent emotional reaction to Zac's surprising revelation about his late wife, she didn't sleep much that night.

The following morning she pondered Zac's parting words for the thousandth time as she dressed for church. He'd bared his soul. And she'd just sat there like a ninny, with her mouth hanging open, and stared at him. The anguish in his expression had made her stomach hurt then—and it was doing the same thing, again and again, every time she relived the poignant scene.

She didn't recall saying anything relevant to Zac as he'd picked up his sleeping son and walked out the door. Now that she'd had more time to think about it, she realized that she should have at least expressed sympathy. If she hadn't been so busy trying to figure out exactly what he'd meant by his shocking confession, she might have. Unfortunately, she'd been so dumbfounded over the whole thing, her mind had gone blank.

"Of all the times to keep my mouth shut," she muttered to herself. "Now they probably won't show up for church this morning and it'll be my fault." Full of self-disgust and regret, she closed her eyes momentarily and prayed, *"I'm sorry, Father. I really blew it this time. I wanted to comfort him but I just didn't know what to say."*

Of course, saying nothing was probably better than blurting out the wrong thing, she reasoned sensibly. Well-meaning people were notorious for making someone's grief worse when all they meant to do was offer solace.

Tina picked up her Bible and scanned the room blankly, wondering why she felt as if she were forgetting something. Nothing came to her, so she gave up and headed for her truck, continuing to ponder the puzzle that was Zac Frazier.

Actually, it was just as well she hadn't openly expressed too much concern. She didn't want the man to get into the habit of confiding in her, because then he might expect her to reciprocate with details from her own past. That, she would never do.

Starting her truck, Tina headed toward the opposite side of Serenity, more than ready for the worship service to come. *"Okay, Lord,"* she said softly and with relief. *"I know if the Fraziers are meant to be in church with me, they'll get there in spite of my mistakes. I just pray they go* somewhere *to worship."*

Almost positive she wasn't going to see Zac and Justin in church, Tina grimaced. They were going to miss the dinner-on-the-ground if they didn't show up. That would be a real shame. The picnic atmosphere would be a wonderful way to get Justin more involved with some of the other children his age, and...

Suddenly, she realized what had been nagging at the fringes of her spinning consciousness all morning. "Oh, no! Dinner-on-the-ground!" The bewilderment surrounding Zac's statement of responsibility for his wife's death had made her forget to fix or bring any food. Well, it was too late now. There was only one thing left to do. She'd have to stop on her way to church and pick up something. Anything.

Wheeling into the market parking lot, she skidded to a stop, jumped out of her truck and rushed into the store. The instant she spotted the rack with all the bags of potato chips, she knew *exactly* what to take.

Chapter Six

Growing more and more disappointed, Tina kept an eye out for Zac all morning, even though Justin had failed to show up to enroll in her Sunday School class.

Mavis took her aside when they ran into each other after the eleven o'clock worship service. "What's wrong, kiddo? You look distracted."

"Nothing," Tina said quickly, scanning the crowd.

"I see you wore your prettiest dress today. Could that be because Zac Frazier is here?"

"He is? Oh, that's great!" Unable to quell her natural excitement, she stood on tiptoe to try to peer past the older woman's shoulder. "Where? I don't see him."

"That's probably because he's out in the kitchen," Mavis said. "At least, he was a few minutes ago when I got my cake out of my car and brought it inside.''

Tina studied her boss's smug expression and began to frown. ''What's he doing in the kitchen?''

Laughing softly, Mavis said, ''Beating 'em off with a stick, from the looks of it. Except for Miss Verleen, I don't think there's one volunteer worker out there who's over the age of thirty. And to think…we usually have to beg the younger ladies to help out with kitchen chores unless their age group is the one sponsoring the meal.''

''Oh, dear.'' Tina grimaced wryly. ''I warned him that would happen. *Now* he's in for it.''

''We could go offer to rescue the poor guy,'' Mavis suggested. ''A few minutes ago, the Gogerty sisters had him practically backed into a corner and Lela Pierce was moving in for the kill. He's probably still trapped right where I last saw him.''

''Great idea. I don't want him to get scared off. Come on.'' Grabbing Mavis's hand, Tina began to drag her through the crowd that was gathering in the narrow hallway leading from the sanctuary to the fellowship hall. It wasn't easy to make headway with so many bodies crammed into such a small space.

''Pardon me! Excuse us! Coming through! Sorry,'' Tina mumbled. Her short stature made it impossible to see most of what was ahead, so she just kept pressing in the right direction. She'd almost made it to the closed double doors leading into the fellowship hall, when the pastor asked for quiet and began to say the blessing. Tina skidded to a halt. The moment he said "Amen," she let go of Mavis, forged ahead, and burst through the swinging doors before any of the others even got moving.

The sight that greeted her was almost too funny for words. Six—no, seven—women had Zac surrounded in the kitchen doorway, barring his escape. They were all babbling at once. Justin was clinging to his daddy's leg in the same frightened way he had been when she'd first met him. Zac might be flattered by all the attention he was getting, but the poor kid was obviously overwhelmed by it.

Tina called to him. "Hey, Justin! Over here."

Letting out a joyful squeal, the little boy abandoned his father and ran straight into her open arms. She crouched down to give him a big hug. "Hi, honey! I'm so glad you're here."

Directly above her, a deep, masculine voice said, "Good morning."

Tina managed to keep from looking at Zac right away. Listening was bad enough. The sound of his voice had made the hairs on the back of her neck tickle and sent goose bumps galloping up and down her bare arms.

Finally, she got command of her errant emotions and straightened, holding the child's hand. "Good morning." She glanced past Zac at the retinue he'd left behind. "I see you've met some other members of our congregation, already. How nice."

"Yes. It was." He paused to cast a winning smile

at the kitchen crew. Three of them waved back. "I whipped up a gelatin-and-fruit salad at dawn this morning. These ladies were kind enough to put it on a serving plate for me."

"How special."

Zac laughed softly. "You don't sound like you really mean that. What did you bring? Cold pizza?"

"Why do you want to know?"

"So I can taste your cooking."

"Why would you want to do that?" Tina was scowling.

"Just trying to be sociable. If you don't want to tell me what you brought, you don't have to. I'm sure somebody else will be glad to fill me in."

"Undoubtedly." She decided to redirect their conversation. "You missed Sunday School."

"I know. We got here late," Zac explained. "I needed to use the refrigerator at the new house to cool the gelatin and—"

"And my *doggie* came back!" Justin shouted gleefully, tugging on her hand. "He got us all dirty."

Zac nodded. "We had to go back to the motel to change into clean clothes. By then, it was almost too late to come at all."

"Oh, my." Tina was struggling not to laugh. "I can just picture that happening."

"No doubt. If that mutt doesn't quit being such a nuisance, I may have to call the dog pound."

"You can't. Serenity doesn't have one."

''Then, what do the folks around here do with strays?''

''Keep them. Find homes for them. Or...'' She glanced at Justin and decided not to put the rest of the thought into words. Instead, she sobered and said, ''This is the country, Zac. Not everybody around here values animals as pets instead of livestock, the way you and I do. What we see as an unacceptable solution to the problem was a necessary element of survival for years. Old habits die hard.''

His expression hardened, his eyes narrowing as he searched Tina's face. ''You mean to tell me they'd just...?''

''Some would, yes, if they saw no other choice. It's a way of life that's been around since pioneer days, and it's certainly no worse than the city folks who drive out to the so-called country to dump their unwanted dogs and cats, expecting us to take care of them.''

''Hmm. I'd never thought of it quite that way.'' Pensive, he took Tina's arm and said, ''Come on. Let's eat,'' and ushered the three of them into the chow line, together.

The touch of his warm, steady hand made her shiver. Everybody was staring. The Gogerty sisters looked like they were about to cry, Lela was wide-eyed and incredulous, and Cheryl Smith, the only blonde in the bunch, had whipped out a lipstick and was smearing it on thick.

That wasn't the only thing *thick* around there, either, Tina mused. You could have fried bacon using the heated atmosphere of female rivalry in that room!

The spirit of neighborliness at their long dining table was alive and well. Zac met the infamous Ed Beasley, whose old car collection had cost the city a lawsuit after he'd moved to a house in town and left the rusty relics behind. Then there was Miss Verleen, one of the older workers from the kitchen, who had brought him a special helping of her homemade meatballs.

Tina spent most of the mealtime either helping Justin cut his food or laughing at Zac's reaction to having so much bounty heaped upon him, whether he wanted it or not. He'd been sitting there eating for as long as she had, yet his plate remained piled high.

During a rare lull in the conversation, he leaned toward her to whisper "I'm stuffed. What do I do now?"

"Why, you've hardly touched your meal," Tina cooed. "What will all your girlfriends think?"

"What girlfriends?"

"Maybe I should have said your *fan club*. It's a good thing your fridge is working, because I'll bet you leave here with enough leftovers to feed you and Justin for a week."

Zac grimaced. "I don't *want* leftovers. Well, maybe another piece of this peach pie, but otherwise, no."

"I knew you'd love it. That's why I told you to take a slice. Eloise made it. She's famous for her pies."

"I hope she's married," Zac said. "I'd hate to give her an innocent compliment and have her think I was making a pass at her."

"Around here, that could happen," Tina told him, her eyes twinkling merrily. "A fella from Harrison bought a peach pie at a charity auction last year and wound up marrying the one who baked it."

"It must have been some pie."

"Guess so. I didn't know many people in Serenity at the time, so I didn't go to the auction. I heard all about it later, though." She noticed that Zac was staring at her. "What? Do I have food stuck to my teeth or something?"

"No, no." He shook his head slowly, thoughtfully. "I'm just surprised, that's all. I remember you told me you hadn't lived in Serenity your whole life, but somehow I got the impression you'd been around here for a long time."

"Nope." Tina was starting to regret being so chatty. He already knew as much about her as people who'd been a part of her life since her arrival. Being that open with anyone was not good.

"So, where are you originally from?" Zac asked.

"Why? What difference does it make?"

He looked surprised, then troubled. One eyebrow arched. "If you and I were just having a casual conversation, I'd say it didn't make any difference at all.''

"It doesn't," Tina said quickly. Her smile was forced. If only she'd named a hometown! Any hometown. Any except the real one.

When Zac leaned closer to talk quietly, there was an unspoken warning in his tone. "As long as you are entrusted with the care of my son, it makes a tremendous difference…to me. The way I see it, if you had nothing to hide, you wouldn't hesitate to tell me everything."

"Oh, really?" So angry she was trembling, she crumpled her paper napkin, pushed back her folding chair and got to her feet. "Well, think again, mister. My private life is just that. Private. So get used to it. If you choose to take your son out of our day care because of that, fine."

The noise level in the room fell dramatically, and Tina realized her outburst was the reason. Her cheeks flamed. Once again, being around Zac Frazier had resulted in calling undue attention to herself, to her reluctance to share details from her past.

Tears of frustration pooled in her eyes. She knew she didn't dare look at Mavis or any of her other Christian friends, or she'd see their sympathy and start to cry for sure. The only way to salvage her pride and continue to protect her privacy was to leave the room. Immediately.

The outer exit seemed miles away as she circled the long table and started for it, her sight blurred by her tears. Twenty feet to go. Now ten. Five. She put out her hand to open the door. *Almost there.*

Just as she pushed aside the heavy glass door and passed through, a shrill little voice filled with pathos called out, "Miss Tina!" and she thought her heart would break.

A short time later, Zac and his son found her sitting in her truck in the church parking lot, sniffling. The windows were rolled down. He handed her Bible and purse to her through the opening on the driver's side. "Here—you left these at the table and I figured you'd need them. Especially your keys."

"Thanks."

"Don't mention it." He reached down and lifted Justin in his arms, then said, "See, buddy? Miss Tina is fine now. She just didn't feel very good so she came outside to get some fresh air."

Tina smiled wanly, hoping to reassure the worried child, then searched his father's expression. "Is that what you told everybody inside?"

"I didn't have to. Your boss took care of it for me. Do you really have an ulcer, like she said?"

"Not that I know of," Tina admitted, making a disgusted face. "Although it's becoming a distinct possibility."

"I'm sorry if my questions upset you," Zac said. "You obviously have a lot of friends here. They all went out of their way to assure me you were wonderful with children. They vouched for your character one-hundred percent.''

''I'm glad.'' Tina fished a tissue out of her purse, blotted her tears and blew her nose. ''I feel like a fool. I'm not normally so touchy.''

''And I don't usually act so defensive.''

''Only where Justin is concerned.'' Tina reached out to gently caress the child's arm. ''That's understandable. I know you love him very much. I just wish...''

''What? That we could spend a little more of our free time together? The three of us? Hey, what a coincidence. I've been thinking the same thing.''

Tina stared at Zac, incredulous. Why would he make a pass at her when they'd both insisted they weren't interested in pairing up? Then she noted the deep concern in his eyes as he chanced a sidelong peek at his son, and she suddenly understood his motives. Perfectly. As a professional counselor he was in his element, in control of things, but as a single father he still felt lost. All he was doing was asking her for more help. How could she refuse when his plea was a direct answer to her ongoing prayers for Justin?

''I suppose we could get together once in a while,'' Tina finally said. ''Since we'll be neighbors, it'll be easy.'' The relief in Zac's expression was so transparent that it threatened to bring back her tears, so she switched her attention to the boy. ''Only, you have to promise to keep your doggie on a leash when

Zorro's outside with me, at least until they get to be friends. Okay?''

"Okay!" Justin shouted eagerly.

Zac began to scowl at her, his dark eyes narrowing. "Now, wait a minute. I never said anything about keeping that dog."

"You did feel sorry for him, though. I could tell. And he has to stay somewhere while we advertise to try to find his owner. Might as well be at your place."

"Oh, sure. No problem," he countered. "All I have to do is get used to dodging his muddy paws every time I walk out the door."

The cynical look on the man's face made Tina chuckle, in spite of her personal problems. "He's just one of God's poor, lost creatures. I have a way with animals. I can teach him to stop jumping on you, if you want."

A smile brightened Zac's countenance, lit his eyes. "It's a deal. That'll be something you and Justin can do together when you visit us." He gave his son a quick hug as he put him down. "Right, buddy?"

The child nodded enthusiastically, holding tight to his daddy's hand. "Uh-huh. Can we do it now? Today?"

"That's up to Miss Tina."

She leaned out of the truck window to smile down at the little boy. "If the dog is still hanging around when we all get home, I'll come over and we can start training him. I promise."

Zac mouthed a silent *thanks,* and backed away with his son, watching as Tina started her truck and drove away. He began to frown. There was something about her that still bothered him. Maybe it was the contrast between her normally loving attitude and the defensiveness he'd glimpsed when she'd gotten upset and fled the fellowship hall.

He took a deep breath and released it as a quiet, pensive sigh. Tina Braddock's past, whatever course it had taken, really was none of his business. Her good reputation in Serenity was unquestioned, unmarred. On the surface she appeared to be just about perfect, from her skill with small children to her beautiful flower garden to her membership in the local church and participation in all the charitable activities he'd been told about that morning.

So, what was her problem? And why did he care? Zac asked himself. *Why, indeed.* Because his pretty neighbor was getting to him, that's why. Beneath the calm surface of the image she presented to the world, he'd sensed uneasiness, foreboding, even fear. But what was she afraid of? What could possibly affect her so deeply that she refused to even tell him a simple thing like where she was from?

He was going to find out what was causing her reticence and unhappiness, he vowed silently. Somehow, he was going to find out everything. And when he did, he was going to use his professional skills to help her face her fears and put them behind her. That was the least he could do in return for her willingness to help his son.

Verleen spotted Zac before he and Justin reached their van. Waving, she called, "Hey, there. Wait up! You forgot your meatballs."

"Sorry about that," he said, pausing politely as she approached. "But I'm sure there are plenty of other folks who can use some extra food."

"Nonsense. Any man with a hungry boy to feed and no wife to cook for him needs all the help he kin get." She motioned toward the group coming out the back door of the fellowship hall. "Over here! I caught 'em in time."

Zac's eyes widened. A parade of women was marching across the parking lot, obviously bearing leftovers intended for him. "Really, ma'am, I—"

"Now, son, there's no need to be shy," Verleen said, giving his arm a motherly pat. "We want you to have plenty to eat." She stepped back as the others approached to present him with their specialties, one by one.

The last in line placed a package of homemade cookies atop the stack of foil-and-plastic-wrapped goodies already in Zac's arms, smiling at him with confidence. "I'm Inez Gogerty, remember? I'm afraid they ate all my chicken salad. Always do. I saved you a few sugar cookies, though." Her smile widened, her expression eager. "I'll drop by your place with a fresh chicken salad in a few days, when you've had time to eat up all this other stuff.''

''You don't know where...''

''Where you live? Of course I do,'' she said, giggling nervously. ''Everybody gets curious when we see a new face in town. We probably knew which house you were renting before the ink dried on the lease.'' She glanced at the others who were still crowded around Zac's van. ''Didn't we, girls.''

There was a twittery chorus of happy agreement and broad smiles from all the women.

Zac was beginning to feel like the star attraction at the zoo. Tucking the tall stack of odd-shaped packages under his chin to steady it, he managed to open the sliding side door of the van without dropping anything. Justin clambered in and climbed into his safety seat, while Zac carefully piled the food on the floor.

''Watch that plate o' beans,'' Verleen warned. ''They could leak a might if they was to get tipped.''

Zac had already found that out, thanks to the sauce he'd noticed on his fingers when he'd put everything down. ''They'll be fine,'' he said, wiping his hand on one of the paper towels he kept in the van to clean up after Justin. This was turning out to be the most unusual visit to church he'd ever experienced. He'd thought Tina had been exaggerating when she warned him about the reception he'd receive, but she hadn't even begun to cover the present situation.

He slid behind the wheel and shut the door. ''Well,

I'd better be getting on home so I can put all this food in the refrigerator. Wouldn't want any of it to spoil in the heat.''

Everyone was still standing there, waving a hearty goodbye, when he glanced into his mirror as he drove away. It looked as if he was going to be eating a lot of chicken salad, and who knows what else, in the weeks and months to come. Like it or not, he was definitely on more than one woman's list of needy single men.

Zac laughed to himself. So, this was what it was going to be like to live in a small town! How bizarre. He supposed it wouldn't do any good to announce that he was permanently unavailable. Knowing human nature, a declaration like that would only intensify the interest in changing his mind, especially if he explained fully.

Sobering, he shook his head. The last thing he intended to do was tell everyone what had happened to his wife and wind up being pitied for his loss. In that respect he could identify with Tina's wish for privacy.

He'd gone over and over the details of the boating accident, looking for some logic, some peace of mind about Kim's death. The water had been unusually swift that day, but she knew how to swim. Their son didn't. So Zac had towed the boy to shore first, then gone back to rescue her. What else could he have done? How could he have known she had hit her head and slipped out of her unfastened life vest?

And now it was just the two of them left. Father and son. Alone. Did Justin remember much about the accident? Or blame Zac the way he blamed himself? Considering the nightmares the boy kept having, both were possible, at least subconsciously.

Zac gritted his teeth in senseless anger. He'd made the wrong choice and there was no going back. Nothing he did was ever going to cure what ailed his family, or make things right again. God help him, there were times when he looked at his son and almost wished...

No! No! his conscience screamed. Sickened by the gravity of his wild thoughts, Zac pulled the van to the side of the road, set the brake and quickly climbed into the back seat next to Justin. His voice broke before he could finish saying "I love you, buddy."

The child, reacting to the intensity of his father's feelings, reached out his little arms.

Without a word, Zac embraced him, held tight, and began to pray wordlessly, letting his tears and his returning faith start to wash away the guilt that had been tainting his life, and his soul, for far too long.

Chapter Seven

Tina had stopped after church to pick up a leash and collar for Justin's dog, when suddenly she began to feel uneasy. Pivoting, she scanned the other shoppers. Most of them, like her, were dressed as if they'd just come from church. Only one person didn't fit. A gaunt, blond woman wearing a stretched-out tank top over shorts was squinting at her from across the store.

Curious, Tina stared back. The woman did look sort of familiar, although she couldn't place where she'd seen her before. Could she be the mother of one of the preschool students? Tina tried to picture her in different clothes, with her stringy hair styled better, hoping that would help. It didn't. Moreover, there was something about the woman's steady gaze that was unnerving.

The moment the strange woman started to approach, Tina looked away and slipped into the nearest checkout line. She knew she should be pleasant to everyone, even if their appearance was a bit off-putting, but this time was different. There was unspoken menace in that woman's eyes. Only a fool would stay to face it without first knowing what she was up against.

Hurrying out of the store with her purchases, Tina kept her gaze lowered, her head bowed, her shoulders slightly slumped. It was when she reached her truck that she relaxed enough to realize where she'd been when she'd learned to assume that kind of submissive posture.

Tina was surprised to see that she'd arrived home before her new neighbors. By the time she'd changed from her good dress into shorts and a T-shirt and walked over to the Frazier house to deliver the dog supplies she'd bought, she was starting to get a little worried. Zac had indicated they were coming here, not going back to the motel, so what could have delayed them?

The stray dog was lounging on Zac's front porch, half asleep. The moment she entered the yard, it leaped to its feet and barreled toward her.

Ready, Tina braced herself. Timing was everything in a situation like this. She didn't weigh nearly enough to overcome its forward momentum and muscle that big a dog into obedience, and she wasn't going to get a chance to win it over through friendship first, either. Unless she reacted properly in the next few seconds and caught it off guard, it was going to knock her flatter than a flitter.

The dog jumped at her, its front feet hitting her nearly as high as her shoulders. Tina raised one knee to meet its broad chest and jostle it without hurting it. At the same instant she shouted, "No! Down!"

Both of them staggered to regain their balance. The overgrown pup cocked its head and looked up at her as if she'd suddenly become a confusing giant. Tongue lolling, tail wagging, it headed for her again.

This time, all Tina had to do was raise her voice and deliver a firm "Down," and it stopped in its tracks. "Oh, good boy," she crooned. "What a smart boy you are."

Circling in front of her, begging for approval, it got so dizzy it almost swooned under her light, calming touch. Tina laughed. "You sure had Zac fooled, didn't you, you big baby? He thought you were incorrigible."

The wide, pink tongue laved her hand. "I know, I know. I'm the boss now." Laughing softly, she slipped the supple, link collar over the dog's broad head and fastened the ring at the end of it to the snap on the leash. "I sure hope my authority is transferable. One of your new masters is even shorter than I am, and four-year-olds don't have good enough reflexes to stop you the way I just did."

She cupped the dog's face in her hands and looked into its warm brown eyes, willing it to understand her words. "If you want to live here, you're going to have to learn to take it easy around the little guy, or you'll wind up back on the streets. We certainly don't want that to happen, do we?"

As if on cue, Zac and Justin pulled into the driveway. Tina straightened and waved a greeting with her free hand, taking care to watch the dog's behavior at the same time. Excited and trembling all over, it waited until the boy was inside the fence, then charged, forgetting that there was a restraint around its neck.

Just as it reached the end of the long leash, Tina yelled, "No!" as loud as she could, did an about-face, and headed in the opposite direction to counteract the dog's forward momentum. Her end of the leash might as well have been tied to a freight train.

"Wow," Zac said, astounded to see the result. "I'm impressed. What do you call that move?"

"Effective," she said, smiling and warmly welcoming the bewildered canine as it returned to her side. "And painless. The last thing you want to do is allow a stubborn moose like this to turn a nice walk into a contest of strength. One or two firm lessons should be enough to keep him from dragging you around behind him. He seems to learn really quickly."

"I thought for sure he was going to jerk you off your feet just now. Where did you learn to do that?"

"In 4-H," she said, immediately sorry to have spoken without censoring her answer.

"Can you teach me to handle him like that?"

"Probably. Do you learn as fast as the dog does?"

Zac gave a wry chuckle. "I doubt it." He gestured toward the van. "I wasn't clever enough to avoid accepting enough food to keep us in meatballs and desserts for weeks."

"Verleen's rubber meatballs?" Tina asked, knowing the answer but wanting to tease him.

"Those are the ones. Must be at least three or four dozen in here. I hate to waste food. Do you suppose I could freeze some of them?"

"Not if you value your life." Tina was shaking her head and grinning. "Anybody in town will tell you she makes up a big batch every couple of years, bags them, and stores them in her freezer. By the time she serves the last of them, they're pretty freezer-burned and dried out."

"Is that why she had so many left today?"

"Yup."

"Why didn't you warn me?"

"Oh, they won't kill you. Not yet. But if you refroze them after they'd been sitting at room temperature for so long, they might be pretty deadly by the time you finally decided to eat them."

"Terrific." Zac gathered up as much of the food as he could carry without dropping it, and headed for the front door. "Justin, you and Miss Tina come with me. And leave that flea-bitten nuisance outside."

"But, Da-a-a-ad…"

"One training lesson is not enough to teach him

the manners he needs to get along in the house,'' Zac explained to his unhappy son. ''Besides, he needs a bath.''

''He also needs a name,'' Tina interjected. ''The only thing I've heard you call him so far is a nuisance.''

''That'll do fine,'' Zac said, flashing a self-satisfied grin. ''We'll call him Nuisance.''

She made a sour face. ''Ugh. What an awful name.''

''Then, you pick one,'' Zac challenged.

''Maybe Justin would like to choose his name.'' Tina looked expectantly to the boy. ''What do you think we should call him?''

''Tina!'' Justin shouted. ''Just like you.''

Wide-eyed, she struggled to control her urge to burst into laughter. ''Um…that's flattering, honey, but I'm afraid it would be awfully confusing, having two of us with the same name. Living so close together, I mean.''

''Oh.'' Justin sulked for a moment, then said, ''How about Mean Max?''

''I like the 'Max' part,'' she said. ''Let's not scare people by saying he's mean, okay?'' As soon as the child nodded, she added, ''Hello, Max.'' Patting the newly christened dog, she carefully slipped the training collar off its neck, then turned to Zac to ask, ''Want me to carry the rest of the stuff in for you?''

He'd paused at the screen door, propping it open with his shoulder so Justin could pass through ahead of him. "Sure. Thanks. About all that's left is a soggy plate of baked beans." When she bent to reach into the van he added, "Be careful. It leaks."

"Yuck. Too late." Tina balanced the plate on the flat of one hand and shook the wet fingers of the other like a kitten with a milky paw. Max took that as a clear invitation to play with his new friend. Free of his leash and collar, he lunged, catching Tina by surprise.

She staggered backward. Tripped. Screeched. Sat down on the lawn with a plop, instinctively hugging the plate of cold beans to her chest, vertically. The thin, foil cover stuck to her shirt while the gooey contents pooled at the bottom, then squeezed out all over her stomach.

In less than a heartbeat, Max went for the food. His bulk and enthusiasm pushed Tina onto her back. Helpless to rise, she rolled from side to side and tried to fend him off with her hands and feet. "No! Stop! Aghhhh…" Her screeching grew so high-pitched it was unintelligible.

Zac set aside the packages he'd been carrying and ran to Tina's aid. He pulled the dog off her and stood there, stupefied. Instead of screaming in pain, as he'd assumed, it looked like she was…*laughing!*

"What's wrong?" Zac demanded. "Are you hurt?"

Tears were streaming down Tina's cheeks, and she could hardly catch her breath. She rolled over and clambered to her feet, wiping her eyes with the backs of her hands. "Tick…" she gasped between bouts of wheezing and rasping giggles. "Tick…"

"Where? I don't see any tick."

She waved her hands in front of her and shook her head for emphasis. "No. Tick…tickle. Tickle me…"

"Oh, for crying out loud. You scared me to death. I thought you were being killed!" Disgusted, Zac let go of the dog. It headed straight for Tina.

Though her breath was still coming in great, deep gulps, she managed to holler "No," and raise her knee enough to remind Max he wasn't supposed to jump on her. This time, she didn't even need to touch him or pull on the leash to get him to settle down. To her chagrin, Zac didn't look impressed with her prowess as a dog trainer. Actually, he looked pretty upset.

"Sorry," she said. "I'm…"

"You're a mess, that's what you are," he interrupted in a gruff tone. "Why didn't you do that in the first place and stop him from knocking you down?"

"Because I *like* wearing baked-bean-flavored clothes," Tina wisecracked. She rolled her eyes for emphasis. "It's my favorite flavor." Looking down, she lifted the hem of her sticky shirt away from her body and saw what a mess the mishap had made of her midriff. A heartfelt "Oh, yuck" slipped out before she could censor it.

When she looked back at Zac, however, she was glad she'd made the candid comment, because the corners of his mouth were starting to twitch up. Tina made a face at him. "I suppose this means you're not going to invite me into your house."

"Can't. I've already returned the carpet cleaner." His smile grew. "You're still dripping beans."

"I know. I guess I should be thankful your stupid dog ate most of them off me. He's probably starving. When did you feed him last?"

"I didn't. I'm not used to having pets. I didn't think of stopping on the way home from church to pick up dog food."

"Well, no wonder!"

Tina could tell that his spreading grin was mostly because of the comical condition she was in. Good thing she wasn't trying to impress him the way all the other women had been that morning, she thought cynically, because right now she looked more like a ruined picnic than a delectable pick.

"If you'll excuse me, I think I'll go home and change," Tina said in an overly sweet voice.

"Good idea."

"I knew you'd like it." She glanced down at Max. "The leash and training collar are over by your van. Would you mind restraining him so he doesn't follow me home?"

Zac chuckled softly. "Why? Maybe he'd rather be your dog. He does seem overly fond of you."

"No way." Tina cast Zac a look of mock disgust. "Feed the poor thing some of your extra meatballs to hold him for a while. I'll borrow a couple of cups of dry food from the Petersons till you can get to the store and buy him a big bag of his own.''

Starting for the gate, she paused. ''And get him a decent food dish, will you? I'm sick of him using me as his dinner plate.''

The sound of Zac's rich laughter was still echoing when Tina got to her own back door and let it slam behind her.

As soon as Tina had showered and changed into clean clothes, she dashed up the street to borrow the dog food and returned to Zac's.

Justin and Max were both on the front porch. To her delight and relief, the gangly, energetic pup had laid down next to the boy, rested his chin on his front paws, and was behaving beautifully. He raised his head when she approached, but otherwise remained quiet.

Holding the paper sack of dry dog food behind her to hide it, she smiled at the pair and spoke softly, maintaining the atmosphere of calm. ''Hi, fellas. What's up?''

''Daddy's painting again,'' Justin said.

''Oh.'' She started up the steps past the boy and dog, certain Max would smell the sack of food and cause trouble. Amazingly, he stayed put, so she asked, ''Did your dad give the dog some of those meatballs like I told him to?''

''Uh-huh.'' The boy laid his hand on the dog's

broad head and stroked his fur gently. "He even let me feed him in the kitchen."

Wow. They were making great progress. "How nice. Was Max a good boy?"

"Uh-huh. Real good. He ate lots. We didn't have to come outside till he threw up on the floor."

It was all Tina could do to keep from chuckling out loud as she made her way into the house. Poor Zac. He couldn't win. Detouring through the kitchen, she left the sack of dry kibbles on the back of the counter, carefully out of Justin's reach so he wouldn't overfeed his new pet. Again.

She located Zac in the second bedroom. It looked like he'd already finished painting the hall. "I'm impressed," she said with a smile. "You've gotten a lot done since the last time I was here."

"I'm getting the hang of it." His gaze traveled over her from head to toe, then he grinned. "You cleaned up pretty well, considering. I don't think I'll ever be able to eat another baked bean without cracking up."

"Good. You didn't seem to think it was all that funny at the time. I was afraid you'd hold it against the dog. He was only doing what came naturally, you know." When she noted Zac's souring expression, she added, "He really is a wonderful pet for Justin. You should have seen them just now, sitting out on the porch together like old pals."

"Did my son tell you I got the chance to use my new floor mop, thanks to that mutt?"

"He might have mentioned it, yes." Tina cleared her throat to stifle her giggles. "I thought you weren't going to permit the dog in the house because he was dirty? You didn't let *me* in."

"That's because you were in worse shape than the mutt."

"Be nice or I won't help you finish painting," she warned.

Zac arched one eyebrow. "Is that a *promise?*"

"Fine. If you don't want my help, I'll go home."

"Okay, okay. You can stay. How about helping Justin wash the mutt instead of painting with me? He's been begging me to let him do it, and I know he couldn't manage a job like that alone."

"What makes you think he and I can handle Max's bath by ourselves?"

"I look at it this way," Zac said, busying himself with his painting supplies rather than continuing to face Tina. "It's a hot day so it won't hurt Justin to get wet, and even if you two make another big mess, watching you struggle with that stubborn dog should be worth a good laugh."

"I ought to wash him in your bathtub," Tina taunted. "You'd probably *never* get the ring out."

"How about using your tub, instead?"

"Not a chance. I'll get a hose and do it outside. We'll need some shampoo, too, unless you happen to have a bottle of flea soap handy."

"Never use it, myself," Zac responded. His smile faded. "I sure hope bringing Max in the house once in a while doesn't mean I'll have to start."

It took some careful planning to bring both their dog-bathing supplies and their unwilling victim into close proximity. Max acted as if the hose were a toy, until Tina tried to wet him down with it. If she hadn't put his collar on him and snubbed the leash to the fence, he'd probably have jumped out of the yard the same way he'd first gotten in.

Justin threw his thin arms around the dog's neck to hold him still. That technique did work, but it also brought the little boy into position to get nearly as good a washing as the dog.

"Let go," Tina ordered. "He's wet enough, now. I don't want to get soap in your eyes."

"I'm not scared," Justin declared.

"I know you're not, sweetie, but the shampoo might sting your eyes and make you cry. We don't want that, do we?"

Backing away, he shook his head. "Uh-uh."

"Good. Hand me that green bottle, please."

Max had stopped struggling and was watching her warily, head lowered and floppy ears folded back against his head. As soon as she poured shampoo along his spine and began to lather it by vigorously scratching his back, he started to relax and actually leaned toward her.

"See, Justin? He likes it." Tina edged aside. "He

just needed to know we weren't going to hurt him. Come closer so you can rub his back, too.'' The child was quick to obey. ''That's it. Wiggle your fingers as hard as you can.''

While the dog was being distracted, Tina went to work on his neck and the sensitive areas of his face.

''Won't he cry, like me?'' Justin asked, concerned.

''I'm being very careful around his eyes so I don't get soap in them. He'll be fine.''

The child was quiet for a few moments, then said soberly, ''Daddy cried.''

Although she was embarrassed to be told about such a private incident, Tina didn't want the boy to think he'd done anything wrong, so she treated his comment as casually as she could. ''Everybody cries sometimes.''

''My daddy doesn't. He never cries—'cept today.''

Tina's gaze darted toward the house. ''Today?''

''Uh-huh. I made it all better.''

''I'm sure you did,'' she said tenderly.

''I did. I gave him a hug, just like Mommy used to do.''

Tears of gratitude and empathy filled Tina's eyes. Many young children had the ability to accept a loss simply, with a pure faith that most adults found so astounding they couldn't relate to it. This was the opportunity she'd been praying for. Her heart focused on her heavenly Father once again. *Please, Lord, tell me what to say, how to help.*

When she opened her mouth to speak, the words were there. "You miss your mommy, don't you."

"Uh-huh. She was pretty." Before Tina could comment, he added, "She died and went to see Jesus."

"I know. Your daddy told me. It made him very sad."

"Yeah. But it's okay."

"Why is that?" Tina was fighting to keep the emotional quaver out of her voice. Clearly, Justin had accepted the inevitability of his mother's death without question.

"'Cause Jesus loves her. She said so. He loves me, too. And Daddy." Looking at Tina he began to smile. "Jesus loves you, too. He really does!"

Turning to him without thought for anything around them, she pulled the little boy into her arms and held him tight. "I know He does, honey. Lots of people have told me that, but I've never heard it said as well as you just said it."

Zac had been listening to barking, screeching and giggling in the yard for the past fifteen minutes. As soon as he was done painting, he gave in to his curiosity and went to see what was going on.

An outrageous sight greeted him. Tina was holding Max on the leash. Justin, soggy from his hair to his bare feet, was apparently trying to hose him down with a spray nozzle, and the agile dog was dodging so well that Tina was getting hit with most of the water.

Incredulous, Zac stood on the porch and shook his head. What a trio. Not a rational one in the bunch. At least he had sense enough to stay out of the melee.

Tina spotted him and waved her whole arm. "Come on in. The water's fine."

"I can see that."

"Your dog's clean."

Zac chuckled derisively. "How can you tell?"

"Because he smells so good. Like lilacs." She had to pause to duck another squirt from the hose. "Take a sniff of him and see for yourself."

"No, thanks. I think I'll pass."

Tina was in such high spirits, she refused to let Zac's stodgy attitude get to her. "What's the matter, Frazier? Afraid of a little water?"

"No. I just have more common sense than the three of you put together, that's all."

"Oh?" She noticed that he had carelessly wandered awfully far from his front door. Trying to look innocent, she edged closer to the porch, crooking her finger at Justin to join her.

"Don't even *think* of turning that hose on me," Zac warned, wary.

"I wouldn't dream of it." Relieving the boy of his dog-rinsing duties, Tina started to carefully run water over Max's back, scratching him into a state of bliss as she worked her way from his head to his tail. "There. See?" she finally said to Zac. "He's a lighter golden color than we thought. By the time he's dry, you won't recognize him.''

"Oh, I'll still know him," Zac replied with exaggerated disdain. "Considering all the *fun* we've had so far, I imagine he's going to be pretty hard to forget."

"In that case..." Before she could change her mind, Tina stopped scratching the dog's back to deter his shaking, stepped in front of Justin as a shield, squinted her eyes, pressed her lips tightly together...and let go.

Max started to tremble, then he shook. Cascades of water flew off him in all directions. The deluge began at his head, soggy ears flapping, then quickly worked its way down his body to the end of his long tail, before starting over at the front.

Zac howled and ducked to try to stay dry, but he was too slow. Spitting and muttering, he wiped his face with his hands and looked down at his water-speckled clothing. Then, he focused on Tina.

The moment his gaze fastened on her, she read an unspoken threat of retaliation. With a shriek she grabbed Justin by the hand and darted around the side of the house. Max was running in wide circles, stopping occasionally to shake himself and obviously enjoying this new game. Which meant there was no way Tina could effectively hide and wait until Zac cooled off. The friendly dog would undoubtedly give away her hiding place. Nevertheless, she ducked behind a bush at the rear of the house and crouched, pulling the boy with her.

What had possessed her to purposely get Zac wet like that? Was it his smug, self-righteous attitude? His direct order practically *daring* her to turn the hose on him? Or did the impulse to raise his spirits go deeper?

When Justin had told her that his father had wept, the simple story had touched a place in her heart she'd thought she'd walled off for good.

Tina chewed on her lower lip. Somehow, someday, she knew she must find a way to gently tell Zac that he'd been wrong about Justin's lack of adjustment after Kim's accident.

Difficulty accepting the loss wasn't his son's problem. If it was anyone's, it was Zac's.

Chapter Eight

Zac's exaggerated growling and grumbling as he searched for them made Justin giggle. Tina bent down beneath the overgrown, purple-flowered, rose of Sharon bush and hushed him with a finger to her lips.

"Shh. Quiet. We can't hide from your daddy if you keep making noise!" She could tell the boy was trying to be still but was having so much fun that it was impossible.

As Max galloped past, dragging his leash, Tina reached out to grab it. She missed. The effort caused her to turn slightly, and she thought she spotted a flash of movement out of the corner of her eye. *Oh, no!* Zac must be trying to sneak up on them!

Tina bolted from behind the bush and took off in the opposite direction. Behind her, Justin squealed. In the split second it took her to glance back to make

sure the boy was all right, she ran full tilt into a solid,
soggy chest. A solid, soggy, *masculine* chest. If the
collision hadn't knocked the wind out of her, she'd
have screamed.

Zac's arms instantly locked around her waist.
"Well, well, what have we here?" he drawled.
"Could it be my troublesome neighbor?"

She pushed her hands hard against his chest and
leaned her upper body back to look up at him. "Let
go of me!"

"I will. As soon as I've decided how I'm going
to get even." He was smiling with smug self-
confidence. "I suppose I could turn the hose on you
but you're already soaked, so there's not much point
in doing that, is there?"

"Just let me go. I promise I won't do it again."

Zac chuckled. "No way. I know you too well.
Even if you don't sic a wet dog on me the next time,
you'll think of something else to do to drive me
crazy. You're…"

As he stared into her eyes, Tina saw his smile fade,
his gaze darken, as if he'd just realized how close he
was holding her. How intimate they had suddenly
become. Any observer who didn't know better would
easily assume their innocent pose was that of two
sweethearts.

The significance of that concept replaced Tina's
rational thoughts. Her eyes widened. Her lips parted
slightly. Staring up at Zac, she wondered absently if
he, too, was awestruck by their accidental embrace.

The answer came without words. Moving as if in a fog, he lowered his head and gently kissed her.

Zac spent the ten minutes following their kiss arguing with himself about what had transpired. The last thing he'd meant to do was kiss his pretty neighbor after he caught her. He certainly hoped he hadn't given her the wrong impression. Nothing had changed. He still intended to raise his son alone. The Lord had taken his first wife from him, and he wasn't ever going to choose a second one.

Muttering to himself about personal stupidity, he realized he'd just taken a big step in that very direction by thinking about being married while considering his blossoming relationship with Tina Braddock at the same time. If only he hadn't given in to his subconscious urge to kiss her!

Disgusted, Zac shook his head, remembering the taste of her lips, the tenderness of their embrace. He wasn't the only one who had gotten lost in the spirit of the moment. Tina had reacted with a lot more enthusiasm than he'd expected, especially in view of her earlier insistence that she wasn't interested in romance.

When he'd released her and stepped back after their spur-of-the-moment kiss, the befuddled look on her face had been impossible to interpret. Only one thing was certain. She hadn't wanted to hang around his place after he'd let her go. Though her abrupt departure had brought tears to Justin's eyes, she'd gathered up her dog-washing paraphernalia and insisted she had to leave.

"So, *now* what do I do?" Zac asked himself cynically. "I've got a sulking kid who's hiding in his room and won't even talk to me, a wet dog the size of a pony that I didn't want in the first place, a house without a stick of furniture in it, and I've alienated the woman who takes care of my son every single day. How much more can go wrong?"

That thought brought him up short. Given the daily possibilities of tragedy and loss, his current problems were insignificant. And fixable. All he had to do was swallow his pride and apologize to Tina.

He was halfway to her house when it occurred to him that he didn't have the foggiest idea what he was going to say.

Zorro was the first to realize that they had company. Arching his back and hissing once, he ran into Tina's bedroom and hid under the bed.

She bent down, lifted the dust ruffle and peered at him. "What's the matter, baby? What scared you?" Zorro stared at her, his yellow eyes wide.

Straightening, she smoothed the hem of her clean T-shirt over the outside of her shorts and began to towel-dry her clean, damp hair. "Never mind. I suppose it has to be at least one of the Fraziers. Poor kitty. I know exactly how you feel. The boy and the dog aren't so bad, but that man scares the stuffing out of me."

Zorro peeked out from under the ruffle, responding to Tina's calming tone of voice. A sharp knock at the front screen door sent him scrambling back into his sanctuary.

"If you're selling something, go away," she called, starting for the door.

"How about if I'm giving away apologies? Free. Would you like one of those?"

The truly contrite look on his face did more to convince her than his words. She kept the screen between them and continued to dry her hair, as she said, "I might be interested. How sorry are you?"

"I'm the sorriest guy in Serenity."

Tina chuckled softly at his choice of the local vernacular for some object or human that was miserably useless. "*Now,* you're talking."

How irresistible he looked, standing there with his hands stuffed into his pockets and his hair all tousled. Every time she saw him, he was more endearing. So was his little boy. As a matter of fact, their resemblance was strongest when Zac was acting contrite. Like right now.

"I really do apologize," he said seriously. "I shouldn't have kissed you. It was way out of line."

"It was terrible," Tina teased, working hard to keep a straight face.

"Terrible?"

"The worst."

"Oh. Well. If you say so." Half of Zac's mouth canted up in the beginnings of a smile. "On a scale of one to ten, I'd probably give it at least a seven, myself. I didn't think it was all that bad.''

"You didn't?" Her lips twitched like his, and she gave in to the smile that wouldn't go away.

"Nope. It certainly was a surprise, though. I had no idea you were going to kiss me back."

"Me? Kiss you? No way!"

"You did so."

"Did not," Tina insisted. She wrapped the towel around her head, assumed a standoffish posture and folded her arms across her chest. "Well? Go ahead. I'm waiting."

"For what? I already said I was sorry I kissed you."

"So you did. I guess I was hoping for something a little more eloquent in the way of an apology. After all, your dog did knock me down and spill food all over me, and your son did douse me with my own hose when all I was trying to do was help him wash the dog. A yucky job like that should have been *yours,* I might add."

"Oh, really?" Zac mirrored her stubborn stance. "And whose fault is it that I have a dog in the first place?"

"Well, don't look at me," Tina retorted. "I didn't tell Max to jump your fence. He thought up that cute little trick all by himself."

"Lucky me."

"Actually," Tina said, mellowing, "I think you

are pretty fortunate. I'm not sure you realize *how* fortunate.''

''If I don't, I'm sure you'll enlighten me any minute now.''

''I might. Do you think it would do any good to try?''

Her question was designed to generate Zac's retrospection without requiring an answer, so she was surprised when he sobered and said, ''I doubt it. I haven't been very good at counting my blessings lately.''

Tina knew she was taking the chance of getting in over her head with her handsome neighbor, but she couldn't just send the poor man away when he was so obviously in spiritual need. She opened the screen door and joined him on the porch, seating herself in an oak swing that hung on chains from the exposed rafters. ''You can sit here and tell me about it, if you like.''

Zac hesitated, warily eyeing both Tina and the swing. ''You sure?''

''No,'' she said, shaking her head and smiling up at him, ''but do it, anyway.''

He eased onto the empty end of the swing, putting himself as far from her as possible. Together, they set the swing in motion by pushing their feet against the porch floor. The slow, smooth, back-and-forth movement added to the feeling of peace and helped Tina wait patiently for whatever was to come. As before, she sensed the Lord's hand in this encounter.

That was all the encouragement she needed to cope with the long silence.

When Zac spoke again, there was a marked poignancy in his voice. "I don't know how to explain it. Every now and then I'm overwhelmed by the miracle that Justin is still with me." He hesitated, staring blankly into the distance as he went on. "Then, when I should be counting my blessings, I get so mad I can hardly see straight."

"Because your wife didn't make it, too."

Zac's head snapped around, his dark eyes flashing. "How did you know?"

"It made sense. I don't think there's anyone who can't look back and wish his or her life had been different. That awful things hadn't happened. Don't waste the happiness you have right now by reliving events you can never change, no matter how often you try to figure out what you should or shouldn't have done."

"I should have been able to save them both when the boat capsized," Zac said flatly. "Kim was wearing a life vest. So was Justin. I knew she could fight the current better than he could, so I helped him to shore first."

Tina sensed he was playing out the accident in his mind, so she gently prodded, "That's logical. Then what?"

"I went back for her. The boat was still upside down with its prow jammed against a tree that had fallen into the river. I could see her empty vest floating off downstream. I dived and dived but I couldn't find her—'' His voice broke. ''She shouldn't have died.''

Putting aside her own concerns, Tina reached out and laid her hand over his. ''You're not God.''

''What's that supposed to mean?''

''Just that I know you did the best you could. Did what you believed was right. No man has any power beyond that.''

''So, the alternative is to blame God, right?''

''If that's what you need to do to get through a crisis, I'm sure the Lord will understand,'' Tina said tenderly. ''I've done it, and He's forgiven me.''

She noted the glimmer of unshed tears in Zac's eyes as he looked away.

''I didn't consciously realize what I'd been doing until today,'' he said. ''The whole thing became clear to me when I was driving home from church. It scared me to death.''

''I understand.''

''No, you don't,'' Zac insisted. ''It's not God I've been blaming. It's not Him I need to ask for forgiveness. It's my innocent son.''

Tina's fingers closed around Zac's as she fought back her own tears. So *that* was why his fathering hadn't seemed quite normal. Chances were he'd been so caught up in his grief, he didn't even know why he'd kept Justin at arm's length. Well, he knew now. And he was sincerely contrite. That was an excellent sign. It meant he was healing.

A lone tear slipped out to slide down her cheek. Zac turned to face her and brushed the drop away with his finger.

"Don't cry for me, Tina. I don't deserve anybody's tears."

"Let me be the judge of that. Okay?" Clearly, he'd solved his problem of placing unearned blame on someone else and replaced it with a big dose of self-pity. Should she tell him so, or had he had enough soul-searching to deal with for one day?

That decision was God's, not hers, Tina decided, more than happy to pass the accountability on to Him. So far, The Lord had done just fine arranging chances for her to minister to Zac. Unless that job was done—and she didn't believe it was—there would be plenty of future opportunities to speak her mind and set him straight.

Besides, she loathed confrontation. That was one of the quirks of character that had made taking charge of her headstrong, teenage brother, Craig, so difficult. So ruinous.

Tina sighed. Boy, talk about wallowing in self-pity! She sniffled and managed a wan smile. "Frazier, you and I are a mess. If we got any more down in the dumps, we'd have to borrow a ladder to climb out."

"You do have a way with words," he said. Cupping her face in his hands, he used his thumbs to gently wipe the remaining tears from her cheeks.

Tina wasn't sure whether it was the compassionate

look in his eyes or the touch of his hands that made her tremble. Something serious was going on here. She and Zac had connected, spiritually as well as physically, and the result was so awe-inspiring, so perfect, it made her question its reality.

Blinking to clear her head and focus her whirling thoughts, Tina forced herself to take a deep, settling breath. If she was dreaming, this was the most true-to-life fantasy she'd ever concocted. Even when she'd told herself far-fetched stories all night long because she'd been too overwrought to sleep, she'd never managed to make her tales this believable. This wonderful. Then again, her dreams had never included a man like Zac Frazier.

She saw his gaze darken and narrow to concentrate on her lips. His head began to tilt slightly to one side, the way it would if he were planning to kiss her again. Her eyes widened. That was exactly what he intended to do!

Tina flattened her palms against his chest so she could push him away. *Do it!* her conscience ordered. *Give him a shove and tell him to go home.*

I will, Tina assured herself. *Any second now. Yes, sir. I'll call a halt to this whole ridiculous game we're playing.*

Only, she didn't. There seemed to be a short-circuit in the communications between her will and her body. There she sat, practically stupefied, while a man she cared about prepared to make his second terrible mistake. The first had been their first kiss.

The second would be more of the same. Unless she stopped it.

The weak protest she finally managed to make wouldn't have been enough to deter anyone who didn't respect her. Fortunately, Zac did.

He got to his feet and backed away from the swing, staring at her as if he'd just realized she was sitting there. "Oh, boy," he said, a bit breathless. "We have to stop meeting like this."

Tina managed a faint "Yeah," surprised to note a strong urge to follow Zac, to slip her arms around his waist and step into his embrace. When he'd left her just now she'd felt empty, as if she'd wither like a thirsty, summer flower and blow away without him there to sustain her.

"I guess I should be going," Zac said. "I left Justin pouting in his room. He's bound to miss me pretty soon."

Thoughts of the lonely child helped Tina concentrate on something aside from her own needs. "When will you be getting your furniture out of storage and moving in?"

"Soon. I brought our camping equipment, so we can sleep in the house tonight," he said. "Justin will think it's a big adventure. Tomorrow, I'll stock up on food—and dog food. I've already checked out of the motel."

"That's good."

Which was the truth, as far as it went. It would be good for Justin to have a stable, permanent place to live. It would be good for Zac to establish a new home and get on with his life. The only one it would *not* be good for was her. Having Zac living so close was going to pose innumerable problems, the most disastrous being the growing attraction between them.

He's just lonely, she told herself. Lonely and finally making peace with his past. Soon, he'd probably realize he was ready to fall in love again, too. Given the choices of available women in Serenity and their eagerness to please, he shouldn't have any trouble finding the perfect mate.

Tina exhaled loudly. All she had to do was make sure she stayed away from him long enough to keep him from deciding he should pick *her.*

Walking home slowly, Zac gave himself permission to broaden his outlook. There were worse things than spending more quality time with Tina Braddock. He snickered. Yeah. Like spending time *without* her, for instance.

What was wrong with him? Was he crazy? The last thing he wanted to do was give Tina the idea he was getting serious about her. He wasn't. Well, he *wasn't,* he insisted. She was just fun to be around. And Justin liked her. There was something oddly appealing about her offbeat character and crazy sense of humor.

Her hesitancy to reveal much about her past intrigued him, too. Maybe she was holding back because she felt she didn't know him well enough yet. Zac's imagination kicked in. Or maybe she was keeping secrets because there was something in her background that she was ashamed of.

"No. No way," he muttered to himself. Tina Braddock was the most honest, loving, sincere, sweet woman he'd ever met. There was no way she could be hiding a checkered past.

"Listen to yourself," he said, shaking his head in disgust as he opened the front gate and entered his yard. "You sound like a one-man fan club. So, she made you laugh and gave you a shoulder to cry on. So, she gets along with Justin. So, she's nice. So what? Lots of people are like that. Why should you go nuts over *that* one?"

A weary Max yawned and got up as his master climbed the front steps to the porch.

Already out of sorts, Zac glowered at him. "Oh, lie down and go back to sleep, you good-for-nothing, useless dog. It won't do you any good to kiss up to me. I'm all out of meatballs."

Max began to wag his tail. When Zac sighed in passing, the dog put his cold nose against his hand and gave him a loving lick.

Zac paused long enough to ruffle the dog's droopy ears and smile down at him. "Okay, okay. I'm sorry. But you're still totally useless, you know." Panting in response, Max looked as though he might be smiling, too. The wagging of his tail increased until his whole rear half was dancing the hula.

"Sit," Zac ordered, testing. When the dog obeyed, he swung back the screen door and held it open. "Okay. You can come in. But one false move and—"

Max disappeared through the door in a blur and left Zac standing there alone. Seconds later, he heard Justin's whoop of happy surprise. "Maybe we'd better make that two false moves," he added to himself. "I have a feeling you're going to need at least one second chance."

Hovering in the back of Zac's mind was the impression that the same principle could easily apply to him.

Chapter Nine

The bulk of Zac's belongings arrived early Tuesday morning. A crew was unloading the moving van, when Tina backed out of her driveway on her way to work. Zac was standing on his porch. The minute he spotted her pickup truck, he jogged to the street and flagged her down.

Reluctantly, she pulled over in front of the van and let the truck's engine idle. She'd made a grave error when she'd helped that man find a house so close to hers. At the time, all she'd considered was what would be best for Justin. Now, she had her own well-being to think about, too. Running into Zac all the time and having to pretend he didn't already have a special place in her heart was exhausting. It was going to have to stop. Her nerves couldn't take the constant pressure. Neither could her conscience.

"Morning!" Zac said cheerfully.

"Good morning."

"Got my furniture."

"I can see that." Tina pointedly glanced at her watch. She didn't want to seem unkind, but she had to make sure he understood that she hadn't been making a play for him the way other single women had. "Well, I don't want to be late."

"Just one thing before you go," he said. "My phone's not connected yet, and I need to call the school to see if an in-service meeting has been scheduled for this afternoon. Can I borrow yours?"

Tina almost laughed out loud. When Zac had hailed her just now, she'd been convinced he was doing it for purely personal reasons, when all he'd actually wanted was access to her *telephone!* Oh, well. It wasn't the first time she'd felt like a fool and it surely wouldn't be the last.

"I leave my back door unlocked," she said. "Help yourself. Just be careful you don't let Zorro out."

"Right. Thanks." Zac nodded toward the house. "Justin's still sleeping like a log in spite of all the noise. I'll keep him with me today if I don't have to go to work." Stepping back, he gave her a quick wave and a smile. "Have a nice day."

"Thanks. Bye." Tina glanced in her rearview mirror as she drove away. Zac hadn't moved, but he wasn't looking in her direction anymore. The approach of a bright red, four-wheel-drive pickup had captured his attention.

Tina's stomach knotted. Her mouth went suddenly

dry. The only person she knew who drove a fancy truck like that was Lela Pierce.

Tina slowed, hoping to delay long enough to see for sure. She gritted her teeth. It was Lela, all right. Zac was helping her down from the high cab of the truck. And it looked like she was handing him a casserole dish.

Refusing to believe she could actually be jealous, Tina insisted, "Well, so what? What do I care?" It didn't matter to her if Zac Frazier was up to his neck in fawning women and homemade food. All she cared about was his relationship with his son, which was definitely improving.

Not satisfied, she began to theorize. Okay. If all that was true, then why did it feel like her stomach was twisted into a knot the size of a Cave City watermelon? And why had she suddenly pictured herself slamming on the brakes, making a U-turn, driving back to Zac's and letting all the air out of Lela's tires?

Zac opened the back door of Tina's house and called to her cat, not terribly surprised when Zorro didn't appear. Cats were reserved like that. Give him a dog any day. He might trip over Max every time he turned around, but at least a man knew where he stood with dogs. They were too goofy, too amiable, to hide their feelings the way a cat did.

He paused. Tina's kitchen was just the way he remembered it. The sink was immaculate, the cur-

tains were frilly lace, and there were pots of bloom-
ing violets and various other small plants lined up
along the windowsills. What he didn't see was a telephone.

Wandering farther into the house, Zac continued
to search, sorry he hadn't thought to ask Tina where
her phone was located. It seemed improper to go
prowling through her house when she was gone—
but what else could he do? He had to stay available
while the movers were still unloading. And besides,
he couldn't go looking for a pay phone unless he
woke Justin and took him along. That wouldn't be
fair. The poor kid needed all the sleep he could get.

Pausing, Zac looked around the living room.
Tina's decor was a combination of styles. All the
elements fit together beautifully. Again, there were
houseplants, some by the front windows, some sitting
in the dimmer corners of the room on stands of their
own. The whole effect was homey. Welcoming. And
yet...

He frowned, studying the room further. There was
something missing. "You came here to borrow the
phone, not to analyze the furniture," he reminded
himself aloud.

Quickly scanning the entire room and deciding
he'd have to move on, he headed down the hallway.
Tina had told him her house had the same floor plan
as his, only in reverse, so it was easy to find his way.
He peeked through the doorway to the master bedroom. Zorro lay curled up in the middle of Tina's

neatly made bed, sleeping. A beige telephone was on the nightstand.

Hesitant to invade her private space, Zac reminded himself that she'd known where the phone was when she'd given him permission to use it. Therefore, as long as her cat didn't get spooked and attack him, he'd go ahead, make his call and be done with it.

Reaching into his pants pocket for the card with the phone number of the school office, he kept one eye on Zorro and reached for the receiver. Suddenly, his subconscious locked on to the elusive missing element he'd been searching for. It was pictures. More precisely, family photographs.

Scowling, Zac systematically scanned the four walls of the room he was in and every flat surface where a framed picture of a loved one might be placed. There were no photos. None.

Forgetting his original reason for being there, he checked the other bedroom, then retraced his steps. A professional decorator might eliminate the personal touch that family photos provided, but that couldn't be the case here. Tina's house was already artistically cluttered. Framed photographs would have added to its charm.

So, where were the faces of all the special people she loved and wanted to remember? Surely there must have been someone, somewhere.

The idea that she might have no one to love—or to love her in return—disturbed him greatly.

* * *

Tina's phone was ringing when she walked in the door at six-thirty that evening. She ran down the hall to answer. "Hello?"

"Hi. It's me," Zac said. "I'm checking my new telephone to see if it's working and give you the number."

"It's working." Tina grimaced, mad at herself for being so delighted to hear his voice. The phone wasn't the *only* thing that was working. Her keen memory was fired up, too, displaying vivid images of Zac and making her recall all the special moments they'd spent together. The watermelon-size knot in her stomach had predictably recurred, too.

"Good." He recited his new number, then asked, "You hungry? I've got plenty of supper for three."

Tina's racing pulse began to pound in her temples. In spite of all her misgivings about seeing Zac again, the urge to accept his invitation was overpowering. She was so exasperated by her apparent lack of self-control that a touch of irritability crept into her reply. "If you're offering to feed me Lela's casserole, never mind."

"It smells pretty good. Is there some reason we shouldn't eat it? Or are you just in a bad mood to-night?"

"I'm never in a bad mood. I'm always sweet and kind, like the Bible says we're supposed to be." She could tell he'd grasped her intended sarcasm because she could hear him laughing in the background.

"Ah," Zac finally said, "the old 'Christians are

perfect' defense. I'm disappointed. I thought you had more imagination than that.''

Imagination? Boy, did he have that right! She sighed. "Don't pick on me, Frazier. I've had a rough day.''

"Okay. Back to the original reason I called. Why not tell me about your day over dinner?''

"I might tell you about it, but not while anybody's trying to eat,'' Tina explained. "A lot of what pre-schoolers do is *not* acceptable mealtime conversation.''

"Granted. So, does this mean you're coming over?''

"Do you have any chairs yet?''

"Four of them. And a table. Very civilized.''

"Good. I'm too beat to sit on the porch steps and wrestle your dog. You did buy him some food, didn't you?''

"I did. And more. He now has a doghouse that looks like a plastic igloo, a bed stuffed with cedar shavings, a food dish the size of a turkey roaster and a watering system with a jug that holds five gallons so he won't run out of drinking water while I'm at work.''

"Boy. When you go to the dogs, you really do it up right, don't you.''

"I try. You still haven't given me a direct answer. Do I put three plates on the table or the usual two?''

"Three,'' Tina said with a sigh. "Just give me ten

minutes to change and feed Zorro. What can I bring?''

''Not a thing,'' Zac said. ''We have enough food over here to last till Christmas. Whoever said the way to a man's heart is through his stomach must have lived in Serenity.''

Think ugly, Tina told herself again and again. *Major ugly.* She was rummaging through the bottom drawer of her dresser, looking for the perfect outfit to wear to Zac's and rejecting each article of clothing on the grounds that it was too attractive. Finally, she settled on an old, faded sweatshirt that was missing its arms, a pair of jeans with holes torn in both knees and worn sneakers.

To complete the transformation, she pulled all her hair straight back and fastened it with a clip. The image she presented when she glanced in a mirror was even less appealing than she'd hoped it would be. ''Good. That should do it,'' she told herself, starting for Zac's with newfound energy in her step. ''At least the man won't get the idea I'm trying to impress him.''

Justin was waiting for her on his porch. ''Miss Tina!''

She swept him up in her arms. ''Hi, sweetie. I missed you, today. Did you have fun with your daddy?''

''Uh-huh. We got my toys!''

The little boy started wiggling to be put down. The

minute his feet hit the floor, he grabbed Tina's hand and tugged. "Come look at my room!"

In the background she heard Zac calling them. "We'll be there in a minute," she shouted back.

Tina knew that having a place he could call his own was crucial to Justin. And it was also important that he be able to share his feelings of joy and belonging with someone other than his father. When he made little friends in Serenity he could invite them over to admire his treasures, but right now, she was the closest thing the boy had to a buddy.

Racing through the bedroom door, Justin hit the floor on his knees and quickly held up a model of a bright red truck. "Look! This one's new. Lela gave it to me," he jabbered. "It's just like her real one."

Tina's jaw dropped open. She snapped it closed and forced a smile for the child's sake. "How nice of her."

"Yeah. She helped me carry all the boxes to my room. I got to ride in her truck, too!"

"Wow. You must have had a very busy day," Tina managed to say.

When a deep voice behind her said "We did," she was so startled that she almost lurched into a pile of plastic building blocks. Staggering to regain her balance and catch her breath, she whirled, eyes wide, to face Zac. "Don't sneak up on me like that!"

"I thought you knew I was here." Looking her up and down, he smiled and raised an eyebrow. "I like the new look. It's kind of cute."

Cute? That was hardly the effect she'd been aiming for. Making a face at him she said, "It's for self-preservation. Every time I visit you I wind up a mess. This time, I'm ready for anything."

"Even Lela's casserole?"

"Well, *almost* everything," Tina answered cynically. "It probably won't kill me."

"Not unless you choke on it," Zac teased.

Tina mumbled, "That could happen."

"I know. I can tell." Turning, he was chuckling softly as he started off down the hall. "Come on, you two. Playtime's over. Time to eat. If you don't come now, you won't get any dessert."

"Dessert!" Justin barreled past Tina and ducked around his father to lead the way.

"Looks like he's finally getting caught up on all the sleep he's missed," Tina said. "How long did he stay in bed this morning?"

"I think it was about ten when he finally wandered out to the kitchen and asked for breakfast. I didn't see any reason to wake him earlier if I didn't have to."

"No in-service meeting today?"

"No," Zac said. "By the way, thanks for the use of your phone. I hated to get all dressed, show up at the school, and *then* find out there was no meeting. Besides, this way I had time to get more stuff unpacked. I hate living out of boxes."

"I know what you mean." She couldn't help noticing the inquisitive look he was giving her as she followed him into the kitchen. Averting her gaze, she concentrated on taking a seat at the table. "It's always difficult getting settled."

"Have you moved often?"

The hairs on the back of her neck prickled, sending a silent warning. Was Zac trying to trip her up? Or was she imagining his undue interest? It could be either. Or both. The man was certainly clever enough to take advantage of any momentary slip of the tongue she might make if she carelessly relaxed her guard.

Tina thought it best to redirect his attention to the feast he'd assembled. There was so much food, it left barely enough room at the table for their plates. "This looks and smells delicious. Even the casserole."

"Thanks. Is milk okay? Or would you rather have coffee?" Zac glanced at a stack of unopened cardboard boxes in the far corner of the room. "I think I know where the pot is. I just didn't have time to dig it out yet."

"Milk is fine, thanks." Tina smiled at the boy. "It's very good for you. I drink it at day care, too."

"Daddy says I can ask Tommy over to play," Justin piped up. "But I can't. I don't know where he lives."

"Well, now that you have a telephone, I can give your number to Tommy's mom, if you want, and she can call you."

"Super!"

Zac delivered three glasses of milk to the table, sat down and began to put dabs of food onto his son's plate. The green beans were the only choice that elicited a childish protest.

"They're good for you," Zac said. "And it looks like they have cheese sauce on them, so I expect you to at least taste them."

"But, Da-a-a-ad..."

Tina couldn't help smiling at the father-son exchange. Zac was getting the hang of solo parenting, all right. When he'd first brought Justin to meet her, she'd sensed that all the boy had to do was pout or cry to get his own way. This firmer approach was a big improvement.

"I'd like some beans, too, please," Tina said, accepting the bowl from Zac. "I know they're good because I can tell Miss Mercy made them. She used to cook for the whole school district, back when it was much smaller."

"I suppose you do recognize most of these dishes," Zac conceded. "I'm beginning to wonder if that church of yours is actually a catering company in disguise."

Tina laughed lightly. "Nope. We just love to eat." Waiting for Zac to pass another entrée, she helped herself to a roll and butter. "I'll bet Miss Tessie made these biscuits."

"Beats me," Zac said. "This stuff was delivered so often today, I lost track. Well, almost." Grinning over at her, he held out a deep, steaming dish with a serving spoon sticking out the top. "I do remember who brought this one."

"Lela!" Justin informed them. "It's got dinosaurs in it. She said."

Tina's hand hovered over the handle of the spoon while she leaned closer to peer at the contents of the casserole. Her eyes narrowed in a frown. "Dinosaurs?"

"The pasta kind," Zac explained. "She figured Justin would get a kick out of it."

"How thoughtful." Smiling with exaggerated sweetness, Tina held out her plate to him and asked, "May I have a tyrannosaurus rex, please. They're my favorite."

"Yeah!" the boy shouted. "Me, too. I want that kind."

"Since Miss Tina knows all about them, I'm sure she'll be happy to help you find some." Zac handed the spoon to her and leaned closer to whisper, "Troublemaker."

Determined he wouldn't best her, she stirred around in the deep ceramic dish for a few seconds before filling the spoon and plopping its contents onto the boy's plate. "I just saw a tyrannosaurus hide in that scoop," she said. "If he didn't fool me, he should still be there. They're sneaky, you know."

Zac muttered, "They're not the only ones," as he picked up his fork. "Well, let's eat." When Tina didn't rush to begin right away, he wondered why, until he saw her close her eyes for a moment and fold her hands in her lap. "Oops. We forgot to say the blessing."

"We *never* do that anymore," Justin told him. "Not since..." His shrill voice quieted.

"Well, it's about time we started again." Zac bowed his head. A few seconds later he merely said, "Amen."

"That's not how Mama did it," the boy complained, pouting.

Tina spoke up. "Next time, we'll take turns praying. How's that?" To her relief, the suggestion was enough to stop the child's protest and preserve what was left of Zac's upbeat mood.

His gaze met hers. "Thanks."

"You're welcome."

"You're very good with kids."

"I'd better be. I spend half my life with them."

"What about the other half? What's that been like?"

She pretended to misinterpret his reference to the past. "It's blessedly peaceful. Serenity is a wonderful place to live, as long as you aren't the kind of person who has to have all the amenities a big city can offer."

"How about before you came here?" Zac pressed. "Don't you miss it? Miss your family?"

"My parents are dead," Tina said flatly.

"I'm so sorry. I know how tough that kind of thing can be. But at least you have your mementos, photographs, that kind of thing."

"No. We...I...lost everything." She could have added more but instead simply sighed quietly. There was nothing to be gained by airing sad tales of personal loss. She'd found that out the hard way. Her brother Craig didn't have any idea where she was because of the new last name she'd adopted when she'd first settled in Arkansas. Nobody from her past did. And that was just the way she liked it.

Tina sensed that Zac was studying her. "I appreciate your concern," she said formally, "but if you don't mind, I'd rather not discuss my past."

"No problem." He shrugged and turned to his son. "Hey. Find any dinosaurs yet, buddy?"

"Not good ones," Justin mumbled with his mouth full.

"Well, you let me know when you do." Zac smiled over at Tina. "Speaking of that casserole, Lela tells me she's originally from Chicago, like me. She moved down here with her folks when she was fifteen. Her dad was transferred."

"Peachy." Tina busied herself pushing the food around on her plate so he wouldn't notice her flushed cheeks.

"I think I'm going to like the milder winters here," he went on. "I suppose this southern climate takes a lot of getting used to the rest of the year, though."

"You'll adjust pretty quickly. The different seasons can be kind of a bother to begin with. You're already used to those kinds of changes, so I wouldn't worry.''

''You mean like trees turning color in the fall?''

''That, and the cultural changes. The first few months I was here I went nuts trying to predict what would be for sale in the stores. I'd go to town to buy something I needed, and nobody would have it in stock. The worst part was, I couldn't find live plants anywhere. I finally figured out that was because it was the middle of winter.''

''Well, you've sure made up for it since then. Your yard is beautiful.''

''Thanks.'' She carefully speared some green beans and put them in her mouth, then went back for more.

''I suppose you were used to working outside year-round back in California.''

Tina's head snapped up, her eyes widening. ''How did…?'' The pleased look on his face answered her question. ''You're guessing.''

''Assuming. There's a difference.''

''Oh, yeah? Well, how do you know I'm not from Florida.''

''Because you didn't act like it when I mentioned stopping there to visit my parents.''

''Arizona, then. Or New Mexico.''

Zac put down his fork and watched her closely. ''I wouldn't expect you to lie, especially not in front of a child. Are you telling me that's where you're from?''

Blinking, Tina glanced at Justin. He was watching her reaction as intensely as his father was. "I'm not telling you anything," she finally said. "You don't play fair."

Zac's eyes seemed to darken, and the deep vibration of his voice made her shiver when he said, "Maybe I'm not playing anymore."

Chapter Ten

Nervous and frustrated, Tina spent the rest of the night and all the next day trying to recall the exact words in her telling exchange with Zac. It was a useless effort. All she could remember was the look on his face and the sound of his voice when he'd said he wasn't playing games anymore.

She hugged herself and paced the floor of the day care facility, thankful that none of the children had arrived yet. What was she going to do? Zac seemed determined to dig into her past, no matter how often she told him not to. She didn't dare confess. Or did she? Would that be best? Maybe he really *was* different from all the others. Suppose she explained exactly what had happened?

"Oh, sure," Tina grumbled. "That would fix things *really* well."

If Zac cared for her, he'd probably insist on trying

to help, which could only make things worse. She couldn't chance hurting Craig. Not when he was finally leading a normal life and had a loving wife and family.

Tina sighed as she considered the other conceivable outcome of telling Zac everything. If he chose not to keep her secret, she'd probably have to move again. Even if she was able to find another job in Serenity, she was sure the rumors about her would make staying here unbearable.

Mavis breezed through the door, spotted Tina and greeted her with a cheery "Good morning!"

"Oh, hi. I didn't hear you drive up."

"I'm not surprised," the older woman said. "You looked like you were a million miles away just now."

"Only about two thousand." Tina took a deep breath and sighed. "Life is complicated."

"It beats the alternative."

That brought a smile. "You're right. I won't mind going to heaven someday, though."

"Well, don't rush things," Mavis countered. "The good Lord gave each of us a special amount of time on earth, and He expects us to use it wisely. I wouldn't want to have to face God sooner than He'd planned and explain why I was there early. Would you?"

"No way. I have enough other mistakes to account for."

"We all do, sweetie. That's what's wrong with

churches, you know. They're full of sinners." She laughed. "'Course, that figures. If we were all perfect, nobody would need to go to church in the first place!"

"I love your logic," Tina said. "I just wish there was some way I could go back and live my past ten years over again, knowing what I know now."

"If you figure out how to do that," Mavis quipped, "sign me up for thirty years or so."

Tina looked away and busied herself straightening the children's plastic chairs. Her mind was spinning. Oh, how she yearned to share her concerns with Mavis and ask for advice!

Pensive, she sighed. Maybe there was a way, providing she was very careful. "Suppose you wanted desperately to do the right thing. Even prayed about it. Only, later you discovered you'd made the wrong choice because you didn't have all the facts to begin with. What would you do, then?"

"Hypothetically?" Frowning, Mavis studied her young employee. "Well, I suppose that would depend upon whether anyone else would be hurt if I went back on my word. Then again, you have to remember that the good Lord didn't give us the ten *suggestions*. He called them commandments for a reason. There's no excuse good enough to swap right for wrong. It either is, or it isn't. Right or wrong, I mean."

"What if it's already too late to change anything?"

"Ah, that's where asking for forgiveness and being truly sorry comes in. If Jesus expected us to go back and fix everything we'd done wrong so far, we'd probably mess it up worse and never live long enough to get it all straight!"

Tina nodded in agreement. "*That* I can relate to."

Zac hadn't casually run into his neighbor since the night he'd invited her over for dinner. The only time he saw Tina was when he delivered Justin to day care, and even then she was usually so busy she barely said hello.

Had he scared her off by speaking his mind? Maybe. At the time, telling her he was no longer playing games had seemed like the most sensible thing to do. Now, he could see the folly of his bluntness. Thank goodness he hadn't told her he thought he was falling for her, too!

Sighing in disgust, Zac entered his office and shut the door behind him, glad for the files piled high in the middle of his desk. Thinking about other people's problems would help take his mind off his own. He had less than a week left to prepare for the students' return. Given the severity of the offenses he'd found in the first few files he'd looked at, he was in for a tough year.

Zac snorted. Good thing the school board didn't know how much trouble he was having deciding how to live his *own* life, or they'd never trust him to sort out the problems of confused students!

His intercom buzzed. He answered, assuming correctly that it was the office receptionist. "Yes, Rosemary?"

"I have a package out here for you, Mr. Frazier."

"Put it in my in-box."

"Sorry." She tittered. "No can do."

Frustrated by the interruption, Zac quickly got to his feet. This was one of the things about small-town life he was having trouble adjusting to. Nobody seemed to think a thing about stopping whatever they were doing to visit, even if they were swamped with work. The last time he'd ventured out of his office he'd been cornered by a Mrs. Fitch, the militant mother of one of the boys he was assigned to counsel. If this was her again, he was going to have to have a serious talk with Rosemary.

Rounding the corner so he could see what awaited him, he began to grin. *Oh, no! More food.* Inez Gogerty was standing at the counter with an eager look on her face. She cradled a covered glass bowl in both hands.

"Here's the chicken salad I promised you," she said with obvious delight. "There's enough for your supper, too."

"Thank you." Zac took the chilled bowl from her. "But you really shouldn't have."

"Oh, fish. What're friends for? Besides, I know how hard it must be for you, working all day and taking care of that dear little boy, too. Jason is such a darling."

Zac corrected her. "His name is Justin."

Color crept up her neck to bloom on her cheeks. "Oops. Well, I was close. They both start with a *J*." Pointing to the chicken salad, she added, "My name and number's on a sticker on the bottom of the bowl. Give me a call when you're finished, and I'll drop by your place to pick it up."

"You've gone to enough trouble already," Zac said politely. "I'm sure we'll see each other in church. I'll just put your bowl in the car and return it some Sunday."

"Well...I suppose that would be simpler." She waved as she turned and headed for the door. "Bye, now. Bye, Rosemary."

"Uh...goodbye."

Looking out through the office window, Zac watched Inez walk away. He was successfully holding his amusement in check, until he noticed the comical expression on the receptionist's face. Poor Rosemary had her fingers pressed to her lips, and her face was so red she looked like she was about to explode. In seconds, she was laughing so hard there were tears streaming down her cheeks.

Zac didn't think the situation was quite *that* funny. He held up the bowl. "Want to join me for lunch? This stuff is really pretty good."

Gasping for breath, the receptionist blotted her tears and managed to say "No kidding?" before she had to stop to blow her nose. "I'd heard you were popular but that's just plain ridiculous. Did you see what I saw? Inez was wearing false eyelashes! It looked like a couple of caterpillars had crawled up her face and died on her eyelids!''

''Really?'' Zac shrugged. ''I didn't notice.''

''Probably just as well.'' Rosemary glanced out the window as she wiped her nose again. ''Uh-oh. Look out. Here comes that Mrs. Fitch again.''

Zac didn't move quickly enough to escape. The wiry woman burst into the office and confronted him, not bothering with a greeting. ''Have you got it straightened out yet?''

''I did look over your son's file,'' he said calmly.

''Well? You can read, can't you? Those teachers last year had it in for my Bennie. He don't deserve to be held back again.''

''According to his transcripts, he does,'' Zac told her. ''There was a period of nearly a year when he was truant more than he was in school. When he did go to class, he refused to turn in any homework. Surely you're aware of that.''

She waved a thin hand at him, rolled her eyes and cursed fluently. ''It wasn't Bennie's fault. My sister was keepin' him for me, back then. She didn't give a rat's... Hey, wait a minute. I'll bet those idiots in the other school sent you the wrong records.'' Glaring at Zac, she leaned on the counter to get closer to him, and her strident tone softened noticeably. ''Sure. That's gotta be it. You look into it for me, okay?''

''I assure you, Bennie will be treated as fairly as

any other student at Serenity High,'' Zac said. He gestured with the bowl. "Now, if you'll excuse me, I have to go put this in the refrigerator.''

"Sure, sure. I need a smoke, anyway, and it's against the rules to light up in here. Gotta keep all the stupid rules. Oh, yeah. I'm a great one for keepin' the rules.''

Rosemary waited until the woman had left, before saying "Whew. That woman's going to be trouble.''

"*Going* to be?'' Zac shook his head sadly. "I haven't met her son but I can guess who he takes after just by reading the teachers' comments in his file.''

"Well, at least he hasn't been bragging about the awful things he's done or how tough he can be, the way she does. I'd say that's a point in his favor.''

Interested in knowing more, Zac put down the bowl and perched on the edge of Rosemary's desk. "His mother actually brags about having a bad reputation?''

"You bet she does. Goes around telling everybody what a rough customer she used to be, like she's proud of it.''

"Could that be why Bennie was staying with her sister?''

"Probably. According to what I heard, that woman's been in and out of trouble since the poor kid was little. No wonder he turned out like he did.''

"I'll make a note to have a talk with him as soon as school starts,'' Zac said soberly. He got to his feet and picked up his bowl of chicken salad. "Come on, Rosemary. I hear voices in the staff lounge. Let's go share this. I want to catch all the teachers at once and find out what else they may have heard about Bennie Fitch."

"It's hopeless," she offered.

Zac silently disagreed. There was always hope. Sometimes it was impossible to see from a human standpoint, but with faith, it was always there.

His thoughts immediately turned to Tina—to his hopes that they might develop a deeper personal relationship. Making her a permanent part of his future wasn't a new idea, it had simply grown from an inkling to a definite goal. The Lord had brought them both to Serenity and arranged their lives so they couldn't avoid each other. The more Zac was around her, the more he was beginning to feel that they were meant to be together.

Now, all he had to do was convince Tina Braddock.

Zac called for Justin a little before five. Tina sensed his presence before she actually saw him. The subconscious warning gave her enough time to find something to do on the opposite side of the room. Her intent was to appear far too busy to stop and chat.

The ploy failed. Peeking out of the corner of her eye, she noted Zac's approach. The only thing to do was face him.

"Justin was very well-behaved, today," she said with an amiable nod of greeting.

"I'm happy to hear that."

When he just stood there looking at her instead of going on with their conversation, she asked, "Was there something else you needed?"

"Actually, yes," Zac said, nodding. "First, I want to apologize for the other night. I didn't mean to upset you."

"You didn't upset me." Tina folded her arms across her chest. "I just think we need to remember that two people can be friends without getting too involved."

"I agree completely. You forgive me, then?"

"There's nothing to forgive." She managed a tiny smile.

"Good. Then, we can have dinner together, tonight."

How had he managed to deduce *that* from their otherwise noncommittal discussion? "I don't think so."

"Why not? You said you weren't mad at me."

"That doesn't mean I think it's a good idea for us to spend a lot of time together. Justin is already getting far too attached to me because he sees me here all the time."

"Is that so bad?"

Tina pulled a face. Either the man was dense, which she doubted, or he was trying to trap her. "Not bad. Unwise," she said flatly. "You were right when you said Justin didn't need a friend like me. If you want your son to be happy, you need to find him a mother, not just a neighborhood pal.''

"Ah, I see." Zac was beginning to smile. "You talk about brotherly love but you don't want to live it. Too bad. I was hoping I could count on you to help me with a youth group I'm thinking of starting."

"A youth group?" Had she dreamed up his romantic interest simply because she *wanted* it to be so? Tina clenched her teeth. What a ridiculous idea! Of course she hadn't. She'd merely misunderstood his motives because she'd misread his mood.

She gazed up at him. "What kind of youth group?"

"I'd like to see it made up of some of the kids I've been assigned to help," Zac explained. "You know. The ones who don't come from homes that teach the same ethical standards you and I grew up with. Kids who're already on the wrong path. If I don't try to turn them around, who will?"

"There's a great group for teens at my church," Tina said. "You could always tell them to go there."

"Once they get to know me, maybe. If I tried it now, they'd think I was railroading them. It'll be hard enough to convince them I can work at the high school and still be on their side."

"I don't know what to say."

"How about telling me it's a great idea and agreeing to have dinner with me so we can talk it over?"

Watching her expression and waiting for an answer, Zac kept smiling. He didn't know who was more surprised about the idea of starting up a new youth group—Tina or himself. Until he'd started telling her about it, he hadn't even considered organizing anything that complicated in his spare time. Not that it was a bad idea. It was a wonderful one. It just wasn't a project he'd consciously planned out.

Then again, maybe the Lord had wanted him to take on that very job. For all Zac knew, God might have planted the concept in his head in the first place. It was not only a perfect task for him, it was an answer to his prayers for a way to draw Tina deeper into his life.

When she said "Oh, all right," Zac breathed a silent sigh. "Good. We can stop at the market on the way home and get some steaks to barbecue. How does that sound?"

"I don't get off work for another hour."

Zac took her arm and started to lead her toward the door. "Yes, you do. It's all taken care of. Mavis volunteered to close tonight. We can leave anytime."

"Whoa. Wait a minute." Tina jerked free and faced him. "I just now agreed to go with you. When did you make those convenient arrangements with my boss?"

"Well…"

"That's what I figured. You think you can talk me into anything, don't you? Well, you *can't.*"

Doing his best to look chagrined, Zac shrugged.

"Okay. My mistake. I suppose I can get someone else to volunteer to work with the kids." He brightened. "Tell you what. How about a temporary commitment? Just until I can get the program set up and find another assistant?"

"What? I wasn't talking about the youth group," Tina said, frowning. "I was talking about being manipulated into having dinner with you."

"Oh. I didn't think keeping company with Justin and me was that disagreeable. If you'd rather come on over after you eat, we can make our plans then. Either way is fine with me." Long minutes passed. Zac had to force himself to breathe slowly, evenly.

"Porterhouse. Medium rare," Tina finally said. "And this is a business meeting, not a date, so it'll be my treat. I'll get my purse and follow you to the store."

Zac decided to let her have her way rather than argue and take the chance she'd balk. There would be plenty of time to repay her for whatever she spent, this time or any other.

He loved a tough challenge—even one as perplexing as Tina promised to be. Now that he'd decided to allow himself to get to know her better, he was starting to view her as more than just a friendly neighbor. That outlook gave him such an enhanced perspective, he felt he was seeing her for the first time. There was a double dose of spunk and wit packed into her small self, and that was only the beginning.

Her beautiful eyes were more green than blue, Zac noted, and her hair looked so silky and touchable, he had to fight the urge to reach out and run his hand along its full length. And her lips? Remembering their taste, he felt his pulse quicken. Even when she was scolding him she looked physically ready to be kissed. Holding himself in check until she was *emotionally* ready was going to be exhausting.

But worth it, he added. Definitely worth it.

Chapter Eleven

The market parking lot was crowded by the time Tina pulled up beside Zac's van. He got out carrying Justin. The boy was asleep, his head resting on his daddy's shoulder.

Tina grabbed her purse and joined them. "Poor baby. Looks like we wore him out today," she said, gently stroking the child's back.

"He always goes to sleep the minute I start the car," Zac told her. "Has ever since he was a baby." They headed toward the store together. "For the past year or so, I think he's done more sleeping in his car seat than he has in bed. Hopefully, that'll change now that we're back in a real home."

"He's getting older, too. It won't be long before he refuses to take naps. That usually helps kids sleep better at night." Tina laughed softly. "I think it's because they're so exhausted."

"Good." Zac turned so she could see his expression and rolled his eyes dramatically. "*I* could use the rest."

She chose an empty shopping cart and steered it toward the meat department. "You said he used to have a lot of nightmares. Does he still?"

"Not nearly as often."

Maybe this was the opportunity she'd prayed for. It certainly had the potential to be. Shooting a silent prayer toward heaven, she decided to speak her mind. "I'm not surprised he's doing so well. I've had a couple of opportunities to talk to him about his mother, and he seems very well adjusted."

"You did *what?*" Zac's voice rumbled low, raising tiny goose bumps on Tina's forearms and zinging up her spine to infuse her nape with an unexpected tingle.

"I talked to him," she said boldly. "Or, rather, I listened to what he had to say. Children don't usually fear death the way adults do. They find it a lot easier to trust God than we do, too. If we tell them their loved one has gone to be with Jesus, they accept it as a good thing."

Following, Zac stepped closer and spoke so quietly that Tina had to strain to hear. "You told him that?"

"No. He told me. Your wife apparently taught it to him. At least, that's the impression I got. She must have been a very special lady. Even after she was gone, her faith was powerful enough to comfort Justin and eventually bring him through."

The melancholy expression on Zac's face made her want to caress his cheek to console him, the same way she would if he were a heartbroken child. When moisture began to glisten in his eyes, she had to look away or she'd have wept.

All he said was "Thank you," but those two words encompassed their entire discussion and assured Tina she'd done the right thing. That was all that mattered.

Zac hadn't offered much advice about anything while they shopped, so Tina had chosen their steaks, then picked out some chicken strips for Justin. "All the kids go crazy over these when we serve them for lunch," she said, holding up the package. "Anything else you can think of that we need?"

Zac didn't answer. He didn't even bother to shrug. She waved her hand in front of his eyes. "Yoo-hoo. This whole thing was your idea, remember? If you've changed your mind, we don't have to do it."

Blinking, he marshaled his lagging awareness. "No, no. I'm still a little dumbfounded, that's all. I can't believe how perfectly God has taken care of Justin, including bringing us all the way to Arkansas to meet you."

Her resulting laugh sounded nervous. "I don't know if I'd go quite *that* far."

"I would."

The intensity of his gaze captured hers and held it. Tina leaned on the handle of the shopping cart to steady herself. She was certainly glad they were in a public place. And that Zac's arms were fully occupied holding his son. If they'd been alone, she wasn't sure she could have resisted the alluring combination of Zac's rich voice and intense, hungry stare.

Time seemed to stop. All they were doing was standing there, looking at each other, yet she felt embarrassed, as if everyone could read her innermost thoughts. She certainly hoped that wasn't so. It was bad enough that *she* knew what she was thinking!

Tina was trying to decide what to do or say next, when Zac broke eye contact and glanced over her shoulder. His expression immediately hardened.

"What? What is it?" She pivoted. All she saw was the normal crowd at the checkout counter.

"At the end of the far line," Zac whispered.

Tina caught her breath. Her heart fluttered. It looked like the woman who had stared at her so fiercely the last time she'd shopped here! Could it be the same one? The stringy blond hair and bony shoulders sticking out of a sleeveless knit top made it likely.

"Who is she?" she asked.

"The mother of one of my cases. I'd just as soon not tangle with her here, especially with you and Justin around. When she comes to my office, every other word is a curse."

"She kind of gives me the willies."

"I know what you mean." Zac stiffened. "Uh-oh. Duck. I think I've been spotted."

The blowsy blonde stormed past Tina and went straight for Zac. "Well, well. You have a boy, too? Good. Then, you should understand why I'm tryin' to help mine."

"I do understand, Mrs. Fitch." Turning to hand Justin off to Tina, he quickly refocused on the irate parent. "Why don't we go outside to discuss this?"

"Why? You afraid to talk in front of your girl-friend?" The woman's hard eyes fastened on Tina. "Don't I know you?"

Seeing the woman up close settled Tina's questions. They *did* know each other, if only in passing. How in the world had they both wound up in the same little Arkansas town? The odds against that happening were tremendous!

"No," Tina blurted out. Lord help her! Near panic, she hugged Justin to her chest and prayed the other woman wouldn't remember where they'd first met.

Zac stepped forward, placed himself between the two as a buffer and spoke to Tina over his shoulder. "Think you can handle Justin and the groceries, too?"

She nodded numbly and clung to Justin as she watched his father shepherd Mrs. Fitch out of the store. The icy look in the woman's eyes gave away no secrets.

Shaking inside and sick to her stomach, Tina pulled herself together enough to place a kiss in the little boy's dark hair and urge, "Wake up, sweetheart. I have to sit you in the basket for a minute while I pay."

The child roused slowly, yawning and mumbling in protest. When he saw who was holding him, he brightened. Tina kissed his cheek and fought back tears as she leaned over to slip his feet through the openings in the shopping cart's child seat.

Justin started to look puzzled. "Where's Daddy?"

"He went out to the car for a minute. I told him you and I could handle the groceries by ourselves. Do you think we can do that?"

The boy nodded. Tina could tell he was still concerned. No wonder. He'd gone to sleep in the van with his father, and awakened in a grocery store with only her for company. Anyone would find a switch like that confusing. He might also be intuitively sensing her inner turmoil.

Watching for Zac, she kept an eye on the outer door as she placed her purchases on the conveyor belt, interrupting her vigil only when she had to write a check to pay the bill. When she looked up again, there he was! Alone. *Thank God!* She pointed.

"Look, Justin! Here comes Daddy. See?"

Zac joined them quickly and leaned closer to speak privately with Tina. "A whole year of that woman, and I'll have gray hair for sure. It's no wonder her boy is so hard to handle. You should have heard her cut loose when I got her outside."

He took over and started to push the cart toward the door, slowing when he noticed that Tina seemed to be hanging back. "Don't worry. It's safe. I waited till she drove away before I came back for you."

"Okay." Relieved, Tina hurried to keep up. If her feet had been racing as fast as her imagination was, she'd have beat him to the car.

As it was, she didn't even remember driving home.

They decided to gather at Tina's house because her barbecue was already set up. It was a good thing Zac had volunteered to do most of the cooking. Tina had so much trouble concentrating, she had to let Justin tell her how to warm the precooked chicken strips.

Max lived up to his reputation of being a nuisance. He parked on her back porch and acted as if he owned it. "I shut Zorro in my bedroom," Tina told Zac as she cautiously stepped over the dog. If it chose to leap up while she was passing, she knew she'd be knocked down, no matter how careful she was. Adding a scared cat to the mix practically ensured an accident.

"Smart lady," Zac said. He poked at the steaks on the barbecue with a long-handled fork. "How did you say you wanted this? Rare?"

Distracted, she was fussing over setting the picnic table, so her concentration wasn't on what he was saying. *Or* on her reply. "Whatever. I'm easy. Just don't get carried away."

If Tina hadn't heard him chuckle, she might not have noticed the double meaning of her innocent statement. She chanced a peek at him. His smile was smug. No doubt he was enjoying her slip of the tongue immensely.

Placing his right hand over his heart, Zac assumed a humble expression. "You have my word, Miss Tina. I will *never* get carried away with you."

"That's a load off my mind."

"I figured it would be. So, where did Justin go? Is he sleeping again?"

"No. We put his chicken in the microwave, and he's minding it for me. I imagine that's why your dog is guarding my back door. Between smelling the chicken strips and knowing his favorite kid is inside with a *cat*, Max is probably on the verge of a nervous breakdown." Tina glanced over at the dog. "Either that or he's already had one. I wish *I* were that relaxed."

"Me, too. I hope he turns out to be a good watchdog, especially where Justin is concerned."

"I don't think you have anything to worry about in Serenity," Tina offered. "This is a peaceful town. Folks here look out for each other. Country people are some of the nicest you'll ever meet."

"You mean like Mrs. Fitch?" Zac asked pointedly.

Tina swallowed the knot that threatened to close her throat. Had he referred to that particular woman simply because she was so difficult to deal with? There was only one way to find out.

"Lots of people blow off steam by talking tough, and nothing more ever comes of it."

Zac concentrated on the barbecue instead of facing Tina, and gave a resolute sigh. "I know. I don't have all the facts yet, but I'm planning to look into her past. In the meantime, I don't want you to let that woman anywhere near my son. She may even be dangerous."

"Dangerous?" Tina's pulse sped faster and faster. She looked so distressed that he put his arm around her shoulders for moral support. "Don't worry. Just keep your eyes open and watch out for the kids the way you always do."

"*Why?*"

"Because, even if I wasn't worried about what Esther Fitch might try to do, I *still* wouldn't want Justin to be anywhere around her. She's a rotten role model. That kind of negative influence can stick with a kid his whole life." Zac paused, studying Tina's pained expression. "It's not just her foul language that bothers me," he said slowly. "It's everything about her. Rosemary tells me she's even been heard bragging about how rotten her reputation is."

Suddenly, Tina felt as if she were being smothered. No coherent thought surfaced to rescue her. No viable prayer arose from her soul to call out to God on her behalf.

She stared at Zac, acknowledging a facet of his character that didn't fit the image of perfection she'd created for him. By telling her how he felt about a woman like Esther, he'd joined all the hypocrites who always judged others without bothering to search for good qualities. They didn't care what their prejudicial attitude cost. All they wanted to do was stick a label on other folks so they'd have an excuse to exclude them from their lives.

Anger filled her, taking the place of all rational emotion. "And you call yourself a counselor!" Tina was nearly shouting but she didn't care. "You've passed judgment on that poor woman without even looking at what kind of person she really is. No wonder you can't talk to her without getting into a fight."

"Whoa." Zac held up his hands in mock surrender. "What's the matter with you?"

"*Nothing's* the matter with me," Tina insisted. "You're the one with the closed mind. I thought you were different. I thought you were intelligent enough to show compassion and tolerance. I see I was wrong."

"Maybe you're mistaking compassion for stupidity," Zac countered. "If I see a thunderstorm coming, I'm going to take cover whether the hills need the water or not. Only an idiot stands outside in a storm and makes himself a human lightning rod when he knows what can happen."

Tina was facing him, hands on her hips, feet in a wide, confrontational stance. "Meaning?"

He purposely lowered his voice and slowed his speech, a tactic designed to calm. "Meaning, there are some things no one can change, no matter how much we wish we could. Our past is one of them. Bennie Fitch's mother is what she is. And it's my duty as a father to protect my son." Zac's forehead creased in a frown. "Can you give me one good reason why I shouldn't do that?"

"What about forgiveness? Isn't everyone entitled to that?"

"From God, maybe. Not necessarily from me. It's a matter of priorities. Justin has to come first. He's all I have left."

The sadness in his eyes touched Tina enough to temper her animosity and give her the added wisdom to grasp a deeper truth. "I get it. You don't think you're capable of granting unconditional forgiveness to anyone, do you. And you refuse to try, because you know the Lord would want you to start by forgiving yourself."

"That's ridiculous," Zac said flatly. He turned away to concentrate on the barbecue, jabbing at the meat on the grill with his cooking fork. He didn't look at Tina when he said, "Call Justin and grab your plate. The steaks are done."

Chapter Twelve

They never had talked about Zac's plans for a youth group after Tina had blown up at him, which suited her just fine. All she wanted to do was hide, thanks to running into her past, head-on. She'd prayed all night that Esther wouldn't remember when or where they'd met.

This mess can still turn out all right, Tina told herself. All she had to do was stay calm and remember that God was in charge. That was a comforting thought, until she took it one step further. Suppose the Lord had been responsible for both her and Esther coming to Serenity? What then? And how was she supposed to avoid the woman in such a small town? The more often Esther's memory was jogged by seeing her, the greater the chance she'd remember.

Believing she was still temporarily in the clear,

Tina went to work as usual. At one o'clock she received a telephone call from Esther Fitch.

"How did you know where to find me?" Trembling, Tina clutched the receiver.

"I've been watchin' you."

"Why? What do you want?"

"Just to talk. Nothing fancy. Come on over. I'll be home all afternoon. If you don't want to run into my Bennie, you'd best hurry."

"No way."

"If you don't come, I'll drop in on you while you have all those cute little kids hanging around. Want them to listen to what I have to say?"

"I can't just leave work."

"You'd better find a way," Esther threatened. "Grab a pencil. I'll give you directions to my place."

The house Bennie and his mother lived in was at the end of a narrow, unpaved county road. Tina was glad she was driving a pickup instead of a low-slung passenger car because the dirt lane was mostly potholes and gullies, the result of rain runoff and ongoing neglect.

Esther Fitch was waiting on the rickety-looking porch, a cigarette in one hand, a tea-colored beverage in the other. Tina hoped the drink was iced tea. She parked and started for the house.

"You're late," Esther said, as Tina climbed the front steps.

"I came as soon as I could."

The atmosphere surrounding them was charged, making the hair on the back of Tina's neck prickle. Nervously, she added, "Okay. I'm here. Now, what do you want?"

"Shut up and sit down," Esther ordered.

The threatening tone made Tina shiver. She perched on the edge of the seat of a metal lawn chair. Obviously, it had been foolish to agree to come way out here without telling anyone where she was going. If she jumped up and made a dash for her truck, would the gaunt woman be quick enough or strong enough to stop her from leaving? She wasn't sure, so she prayed for God's guidance and waited to see what would happen next.

Esther was staring at her, shaking her head and cursing under her breath. "You might as well stop pretending you don't know me."

So, the game was over. "All right," Tina said, managing to keep her voice from quavering. "But it won't do you any good to try to blackmail me. I don't have much money."

"I don't want your money. Not that I wouldn't take a little if you twisted my arm." Esther stepped closer. "All I want is for you to have a talk with your boyfriend—get him to let my boy go on to the twelfth grade so he can graduate with his friends."

"*That's* why you made me come out here?" Tina was flabbergasted. "That's all?"

"It's plenty to a teenager," Esther said. She blew smoke in Tina's face. "Bennie would of done fine if

I hadn't been away his whole junior year. It ain't his fault he got behind in school. You talk to Frazier. He can fix it.''

Wide-eyed, Tina gaped at her. "I can't do that. I *won't* do it."

"If you don't, I'll tell the world just who and what you are and where we met, missy." Grinning broadly she stepped back to look Tina up and down. "I'll bet your holier-than-thou friends will sing a different tune when they hear you're a jailbird!"

Oh, how she hated that expression! Tina was desperate to find some way of escape from the inevitable. "It won't do me any good to try to influence Zac," she insisted. "We aren't close friends. We're just neighbors. Why should he listen to anything I say?"

"Not close? Hah! I saw you two in the store together, saw how he looked at you. You might be able to fool some folks, but you can't fool me. That man's in love with you. I'll bet you've got it bad for him, too."

"You're wrong," Tina said firmly, loudly. "There's nothing between us. Absolutely nothing."

"Okay." She shrugged her bony shoulders. "In that case, you won't care if I start out by tellin' *him* I know you from when we were both in prison. It should be a real interesting conversation, don't you think?"

"Don't... Please don't do that."

"Okay. Then, this is how it's going to be. You

want a favor from me, you need to get busy and earn it.''

''You'll only be hurting your son in the long run if you try to interfere,'' Tina argued. ''He needs to be held responsible for his grades.''

Esther wasn't impressed. ''I'll give you a week to see that Bennie gets put back with his old class. After that…''

After that, Tina thought, *I'll need to leave Serenity and find some other place to start over. Someplace where no one knows me. Just like twice before.*

Heartbroken, she gave up and headed for her truck. Was she never going to finish paying for the lie she'd told to protect her brother? It had seemed like such an inconsequential act at the time. One little lie.

Just one little lie.

Exhausted, Zac was glad to see the first week of school come to an end. He'd been too engrossed in his new job to do anything aside from eat, sleep and work. After the first couple of days, Tina had offered to take Justin to day care with her every morning, so Zac wouldn't have to. Since he finished his workday earlier than she did, he always drove the boy home.

He hadn't had an in-depth conversation with Tina since the night she'd gotten so mad at him over his comments about Esther Fitch. In retrospect, he had to admit his pretty neighbor was right. He had been judging the Fitch woman on past offenses, which was a pretty easy thing to do, considering her current erratic temperament and colorful way of expressing herself.

Tina's personal observations about him, however, were a lot harder to deal with. Even if there was a touch of truth in her theory, he didn't intend to bother God about it. After all, Zac reasoned, it was perfectly natural for him to continue to lament the decision he'd made after the boat had capsized. Anyone would. Life was full of missed chances and false starts. A man who claimed he was never sorry about anything he'd said or done was either a liar or a fool.

One of the reasons Zac looked forward to picking up his son every afternoon was that it meant he'd get to see Tina. It wasn't enough that they were neighbors and friends. He wanted more. Needed more. She'd made a permanent place for herself in his heart before he'd even realized he was beginning to care. That was why her criticism of him, personally, had been so hard to take.

Opening the door to the day care building, he began to smile at the happy noises that welcomed him. The place always sounded like a bunch of munchkins were holding a party. It smelled like paint, plastic and whatever the lunch entrée had been. Today, it had *definitely* been spaghetti.

Zac paused and scanned the room, looking for the two most important people in his life. Justin was close by. Tina wasn't. The boy was engrossed in the structure of wooden blocks he was building with

Tommy. He didn't even look up until Zac called, "Hey, buddy. You about ready to go home?"

Reluctantly, Justin went to his father. When he was close enough, Zac reached out and tousled the boy's hair. "So, did you have a nice day?"

"I guess."

Immediately concerned, Zac crouched down and touched his son's forehead. "No fever. Are you feeling all right?"

"Uh-huh."

"Then, what's wrong? Why are you acting so sad?"

"Miss Tina left."

"She did?" Straightening, Zac looked around the large, open room once more. No wonder he hadn't spotted Tina when he'd arrived. What could be wrong? She'd looked fine when she'd stopped to pick up his son that morning. Maybe she'd come down with a bug since then. "Was she sick?" he asked.

"I dunno. She just left." Justin pointed to a tall, blond woman who was busy straightening some toys on shelves. "That's Miss Vicki. She's mean."

Zac took him by the hand and led him toward the nursery area, looking for Mavis. "Come on. We'll go find out what happened to Miss Tina."

The nursery door was ajar, saving him from having to decide whether to knock and chance waking the babies. He peeked inside. "Excuse me?"

Mavis instinctively assessed Justin's mood, then asked, "Is there a problem, Mr. Frazier?"

"No. Everything's fine...I think. I was just wondering— Where's Tina? I mean, Ms. Braddock."

"Hang on. We'll talk out there." The older woman quickly joined him and pulled the nursery door shut behind her. "Okay. What do *you* know?"

"About Tina?"

Nodding, Mavis pressed her lips into a thin line and folded her arms across her chest. "Yes. She's been acting strange lately. Distracted. Like she had something important on her mind. I thought you two might have had a fight or something."

"She did get pretty mad at me the other night," Zac admitted, "but I've seen her since then and she's seemed fine. I don't think she's still upset." He paused to review their past meetings. "We haven't really had an opportunity to discuss much of anything since school started."

"She didn't go to see you today?"

"No. Why would you think that?"

"Because she was acting evasive. She got a phone call, then asked me for time off. You're all she's talked about, lately, so I figured it had to have something to do with you." Mavis smiled down at Justin. "You and the little guy here. If you two ever need a cheering section, call Tina. She's had lots of practice."

To Zac's chagrin, he felt a blush warm his face. "We like her, too."

"Is that *all* you feel for her?"

"No." His sense of embarrassment refused to go

away, so he dealt with it and kept talking. "It's much, much more. Only, please don't tell Tina, okay? The minute I tried to get her to consider a serious relationship, she started to avoid me. I really think we're right for each other. I just don't want to move too fast. I want to marry her, not chase her away. She's a very special lady."

"I agree." Mavis's wide grin crinkled the corners of her eyes, and her enthusiasm made them sparkle. "You can count me as being on your side. I've given Tina the whole afternoon off, so I doubt she'll come back here. Why don't you go on home. I'm sure she'll show up at her place before too long."

"Thanks." Zac vigorously shook the older woman's hand.

She leaned closer to whisper, "Remember, I get invited to the wedding."

Zac chuckled nervously. "I sure hope I do, too."

Tina saw both Fraziers sitting on their front porch steps when she drove into her own driveway. Max was chasing a ball one of them had thrown. The picture of a happy family nearly broke her heart. She hadn't been forced to admit how deeply she loved Zac and his son until today.

The idea of leaving Serenity—of leaving Zac—was unthinkable. Yet what choice did she have? Now that Esther knew who she was, it was only a matter of time before the woman told someone, who told someone, who told someone else. The result was inevitable. At best, all Tina could hope for was the week's time Esther had promised to allow her.

One week. Was it fair to dream of spending every spare minute with Zac? Was it right to pretend everything was going to be fine and lead him on? Tina shook her head sadly. No. She couldn't do that. No matter how much she yearned to be with him, to make fond memories that would comfort her someday, she couldn't take the chance of hurting Zac. Or Justin. She loved them too dearly.

The only sensible thing to do was continue to keep her distance and pray that Zac was not already in love with her. Tina's aching heart refused to allow such a prayer. She *did* want him to love her. She wanted to love him in return. And most of all, she wanted to find a way to banish the old mistakes that kept coming back to haunt her. That was the most unattainable part of her dream.

She'd changed clothes and was pouring herself a glass of iced tea when there was a tentative knock on her back door. Zorro bristled and hissed.

Tina immediately saw why. Both Justin and Max were peering at her through the screen door, while Zac waited at the foot of the porch steps. Justin was licking an orange Popsicle and holding up something small that was wrapped in white paper.

She couldn't bring herself to ignore the boy or send him away, so she smiled wistfully. "Hi, honey. What'cha got?"

"One for you," he said eagerly. "I think it's

cherry. Daddy wouldn't let me look 'cause this dumb ol' dog keeps tryin' to lick it, and he said you wouldn't like that.''

''They do taste better without dog lips on them,'' Tina said, feigning seriousness. She started to open the screen door to accept the treat. ''Thank you.''

Before Justin could hand her the Popsicle, Max barged through the door—headed straight for the cat!

''No!'' Tina shrieked.

Zorro didn't need a warning. He zoomed around the corner into the hallway so fast that his black-and-white image blurred. The big dog chasing him was far less agile. Its nails clattered and scraped against the tile floor as it scrambled to overcome forward momentum and negotiate the same quick turn the cat had made. Instead, it began to slide sideways, feet still paddling, and crashed into the side of the refrigerator with a *thunk*.

That caused enough delay for Tina to throw her arms around the dog's neck and gain temporary control. At least poor Zorro had plenty of favorite places to hide. The only thing that worried her was keeping the excited dog from tearing through her house in a frenzy and knocking over all her plants and knick-knacks while he pursued his quarry.

Zac quickly came to her rescue. He burst through the back door, slid to a dead stop in the center of her kitchen, stared for a second, then exploded into laughter.

Tina was not amused. She'd had to drape herself

across the dog's back to keep him from getting to his feet, and her arms were aching from holding on so tightly.

"I thought..." Zac gasped for breath. "I thought something *terrible* had happened."

"It nearly did," she snapped. "Your dog tried to have Zorro for lunch."

"Dinner," Zac said. "It's too late for lunch."

"I stand corrected." Tina didn't dare let go. She glowered up at Zac. "Are you going to help me, or are you just going to hang around and make jokes?"

That started him chuckling again. "Okay, okay. I'll help. I take it you aren't trying to ride the dog, so you must be restraining him. Right?"

"No kidding. If I let him get up, he'll wreck my house, not to mention my poor cat. Why isn't he wearing his collar?"

"The one you bought for training?"

"No. The red one that buckles on."

"Ah." Zac had crossed to stand beside her. "We think he ate that one. Justin found a little piece of it in the yard. We still don't know what happened to the buckle, but I can guess."

"Me, too," Tina said. "As big as he is, I don't think it'll hurt him, though." She nodded toward a nearby cabinet. "We need a rope or something. I think there's some old clothesline in there."

"I'll see." Zac quickly located the bundle and displayed it proudly. "Got it." He made a slipknot, formed a loop and put it over Max's head before saying, "Okay. I've got him under control. You can let go."

Moving slowly, Tina eased back into a crouch. Sensing impending freedom, the dog lurched to his feet and sent her sprawling.

She couldn't squelch the loud "Ouch!" that escaped, but she did manage to keep from rubbing the spot that hurt the most. Fuming, she sat flat on the floor and glared up at Zac. "If you laugh, so help me, I'll...I'll..."

He held up his free hand as if swearing an official oath. "I promise I'm not going to laugh at you."

Tina could see the corners of his mouth twitching as he fought to keep his promise. Justin was standing right behind him, holding high his melting Popsicle, while the dog licked at the sticky, sweet drops running all the way from his fist to his armpit.

Zac was in passable command of his emotions, until he heard his son begin a high-pitched giggle. That was all it took to push him over the edge of his tenuous self-control. By the time Tina got to her feet, the man was roaring.

The hilarity was contagious. Unable to keep a straight face, she laughed along till tears rolled down her cheeks and she was doubled over.

Finally, she pointed at Max. "Will you please... take *that* out of my kitchen?"

"Sure." Zac wiped his eyes as he started to lead his dog to the door. "I don't know why you invited him inside in the first place."

"*Invited* him?" Waving her hands, Tina loosed another spate of laughter, then grabbed her ribs. "Oooh. Ouch."

"You okay?"

"I'm fine...just...a stitch in my side."

"Maybe you hurt yourself when you wrestled the dog," he speculated. "Hold on a sec. I'll be right back."

"No!" Disgruntled, she watched him shepherd both dog and boy out the door and latch the screen so they couldn't reopen it on their own. "You're not listening to me, Zac. I said, I'm fine."

He marched back to her like a man on a mission. "I heard you. You're fine. Now, lift your arms so I can take a look at those ribs."

"No way, mister. Hands off. You're no doctor."

"I have studied first aid," Zac countered. "And I wasn't asking you to take your clothes off. Just stop hugging yourself, put your arms up and hold still. This won't take a minute. Turn around."

Tina gladly turned her back on him. Anything was better than having to meet his gaze and wonder if she was giving away the secret of her love for him. Did he already know? If he was as sensitive to her moods as she was to his, he probably suspected. After all, he was trained to be perceptive.

At the touch of Zac's hands on her shoulders, she shivered. He froze. "Did I hurt you?"

"No."

"Then, relax. I'll be gentle," he said as he began

to press his thumbs against her spine and splay his fingers along both sides, working his way down. "Tell me if you feel anything."

Feel anything? Oh, yes! But those feelings had no relation to her fall.

It was all Tina could do to keep from moaning with pleasure at Zac's deft, tender strokes. In the loving caress of his hands lay the ultimate answer to her question about his emotional involvement. With a heartfelt sigh, she closed her eyes, accepted the full truth of what she was sensing and leaned back against his chest.

Zac didn't hesitate. His arms encircled her. Held her. She felt his warm, sweet breath tickle her ear, her cheek. Felt the press of his lips against her temple. *This is all wrong,* she told herself, over and over. Knowing her conclusion was the right one wasn't enough to make her pull away from him.

"Oh, Tina," he murmured against her hair. "Tina."

Laying her arms on top of his, she swayed within their mutual embrace. Zac hadn't touched her anywhere he shouldn't have, yet she was completely his. How could this have happened? How could she have let it? She'd vowed to stay away from him for his sake, to give him up without revealing how much she loved him *because* she loved him.

Well, it was too late for all that now. There was no way to go back and undo what had just happened. Even if she broke her solemn promise to God and purposely told another lie, she'd never be able to convince Zac she didn't share his affection. Which meant she had only the pure truth to work with. Truth could hurt. It could also heal. She just wasn't sure how she was going to tell one from the other until it was too late.

Steeling herself for the inevitable, Tina turned around, determined to tell Zac everything about her past. But at the last instant she lost her nerve. Flattening her palms against his chest, she bowed her head and prayed silently, *Oh, Father, You know what a mess I've made of my life. Help me. Please. I don't want to lose him but I don't want to hurt him, either. I don't know what to do. I'm really scared.*

Zac pulled her close. He began to caress her hair with his hand—and her soul with his voice. "It'll be okay. We'll make it work. Don't be afraid, honey."

Struggling for self-control, Tina blinked back tears and drew a shuddering breath. Zac deserved to know all about her before he said any more. As soon as she got her emotions under better control, she was going to sit him down and make him listen to her whole story, even if he resisted.

A yowl from the backyard made them jump apart in unison. Zac recovered first. "What the—?"

"Sounds like Justin!" Tina headed for the door.

Zac beat her outside and leaped off the porch. He reached his son in two long strides and bent over him. "What's wrong?"

"My Popsicle stick," the boy wailed. "I was gonna save it to make a boat."

"Hey, no problem." Zac whistled in relief. "You can save the stick."

The child stamped his foot and began to pout. "No, I can't. It's all gone. Max ate it!"

Chapter Thirteen

"It was after closing time but I spoke to the vet's assistant," Tina told Zac. "She said we should watch him and not panic. Dogs eat weird stuff all the time. We're supposed to call their emergency number if he starts to act funny over the weekend."

"Humph. How will we know the difference? That dog always acts funny."

"True."

Zac was holding on to the makeshift leash that was still around Max's neck. "So, want to walk us home?"

"No."

"Oh, come on. It's either that or replant your entire garden after a boy and his dog get through remodeling it for you. My yard was already pretty trashed when I moved in, so they can't hurt anything over there. We can sit outside and watch the monsters play. It's probably more interesting than whatever's on TV.''

''Probably.'' She sighed. ''Well, okay. For a little while. I don't know if I'll be very good company, though. I'm really tired tonight.''

''You were wonderful company a minute or so ago,'' Zac offered. ''At least *I* thought so.''

She took a mock swipe at him and pulled a face. ''Could we forget about that?''

''Not a chance, lady.''

''That's what I was afraid of.'' Following Zac and Max down the street, Tina felt Justin take her hand, and she turned her most loving smile on him in spite of his gummy fingers. ''Hi, sweetie. Do you know you're all sticky?''

''Uh-huh. My Popsicle melted.''

''I know. I saw. They're really messy.'' Another thought struck her. ''Whatever happened to the one you brought over for me?''

The boy reached into his pocket and withdrew a packet of white plastic. Two hard bumps showed where the sticks were. The rest jiggled and pooled in the lowest point. Tina stifled a grin.

''I'm afraid it melted.''

''That's okay.'' Justin held his gift up to her with solemn dignity. ''You can put it back in the freezer and eat it later.''

Zac took the drippy mess for her, grasping its edge between his thumb and forefinger and holding it at arm's length. ''I'll refreeze it for you, Miss Tina.''

His mischievous wink was carefully aimed at her alone. "I have lots of them in my freezer, so it won't be lonesome."

The little boy rolled his eyes. "Da-a-a-ad, food doesn't get lonesome."

"Oh, sorry," Zac said. "My mistake."

He opened the gate to his yard and led the way with Max, not releasing the excited canine until they were all safely inside. As soon as he was loose, the dog galloped off with Justin in hot pursuit.

Tina couldn't help being amused at the father-son exchange. "Imagine that. A grown man not knowing that food doesn't get lonesome."

"Yeah. I can't win. That kid learns something new every day. He's growing up a lot faster than I thought he would."

"They all do. Children learn at a more rapid rate when they're little than at any other time in their lives. Think about it. They have to figure out how to move their bodies where they want them to go *and* master language in their first few years—all with no base of prior knowledge to build on. It's a phenomenal challenge."

"I'd never thought of it quite like that." Zac dropped the melted Popsicle into the trash, then led the way to his backyard and unfolded two mesh lawn chairs, placing them in the shade of a native oak.

Tina sat down and settled back to watch Justin and Max playing keep-away. "You know, that's really a great dog," she observed, not trying to hide her admiration.

Zac coughed and cleared his throat noisily. *"That?"*

"Yes. See how careful he is? He never bumps into Justin and he never leaves him too far behind, either. If that were you or me out there, instead of a child, Max would probably flatten us."

"I still may never forgive him for interrupting us a few minutes ago," Zac drawled, arching his eyebrows and looking at her sideways, teasing. "Want to go into the house with me? I didn't finish checking your sore ribs."

"Oh, yes, you did. I suspect the Lord may have used that dog to rescue us from each other."

"Hah! I didn't need rescuing," he insisted. Breaking into a wry smile, he added, "Of course, maybe *you* did."

"I considered that possibility." Blushing, Tina knew she should take advantage of his good mood to bring up her past. When she searched her heart for the abundant determination she'd had earlier, however, she found little of it left.

Relieved, she rationalized, *It wasn't the right time to confess, and God stopped me. Okay. I'll just wait till He gives me another chance and then I'll speak up.*

The concept of actually explaining everything to Zac sounded easy until she began to think seriously about doing it. Reality hit her hard and fisted in the pit of her stomach. Where could she start? Where *should* she start? If she didn't choose every word carefully, Zac might get so upset he'd stop listening before she got around to the most important details. That was exactly what had happened with her other so-called friends in the past.

Moreover, what in the world should she do—or not do—till the Lord cleared the way for her to confess? Now that she and Zac had quit pretending there were no romantic feelings between them, all she wanted was to be near him. *Very* near him. The pink color in her cheeks deepened.

Zac had been watching her. "Hey. You're blushing. Want to tell me what you're thinking about?"

"Not a chance, mister."

With a smug grin he leaned back in his chair and laced his fingers behind his head. "That good, huh? Thanks. I'm flattered."

"Well, don't get a swelled head," Tina countered. "You weren't the only thing on my mind."

"Oh? Is there something or somebody else you want to tell me about?" Zac brought himself forward, leaning his elbows on his knees and giving her his full attention.

"I...not yet." Tina refused to meet his gaze. "I will soon. I promise."

He reached for her hand and clasped it in both of his, his thumbs skimming across her skin in a simple caress. "You don't have to worry about leveling with me, honey. Don't you know that?"

Not worry? *Hah!* Tina immediately thought of lots of good reasons to worry. Zac might hate her. Or be afraid she'd be a bad influence on his son. Worst of all, getting serious about her could ruin his whole life! That last conclusion was a doozy—one she'd managed to put out of her mind when she'd been fool enough to imagine a happy future with Zac. Well, it was back with a vengeance. Whether she liked it or not, he'd never realize his dream of becoming a Youth Pastor if he chose a jailbird for a wife. No one would hire him under those circumstances. And she didn't blame them.

Tina sighed and forced herself to look at him so she could spot the slightest reaction. "You once told me you wanted to be part of a ministry. Is that still your goal?"

The enthusiasm brightening his eyes seemed to shine all the way to his soul, telegraphing his answer. When Zac began to explain, she felt worse than before.

"I'd love it," he said. "So will you, honey. We'll make a great team. You'll see." He sobered and gazed at her with undisguised longing. "And while we're on the subject of love—I love you, Tina. I was going to put off asking you this until I was sure how you felt, but I can't stand the suspense. We belong together. Will you marry me?"

Watching her eyes widen and her lips part, Zac waited for her to throw herself into his arms and promise to love him forever, the way Kim had when he'd proposed to her. Long seconds passed. He saw Tina's eyes begin to glisten as tears tipped over her lower lashes and trickled down her cheeks. Her lower lip trembled.

Zac held tight to her hand so she couldn't run away, and tried desperately to undo his mistake. "Don't say no, honey. Please, don't say no. Don't say anything right now. Just think about it. Take your time. Take all the time you want. I won't push you to decide. I promise I won't."

Tina nodded and sniffled, trying to smile. Her course had suddenly become clear; the answer she must give, obvious. "I know exactly how much time I'll need," she said, almost whispering. "Give me eight days."

The odd length of time puzzled him. *Eight days? Why not a week?* Zac was intrigued, yet wary. Tina must have a good reason for specifying exactly eight days. But what could it be?

Zac subdued a reckless urge to question her further. "Okay. No problem. Eight days is fine."

"Good. Then, I'd better be getting home."

"Already? You just got here." It was hard to convince himself to release her hand when she stood up and pulled away. Feeling instantly bereft without her touch, he shoved his hands into his pockets to quell the temptation to reach for her again. "Would you like a cold drink before you go? I can make some lemonade. Iced tea? I know, I'll get you a fresh Popsicle! What flavor would you like? I think we have cherry, orange, and maybe grape."

"No. Nothing, thanks." Head down, heart heavy, she started for home.

Zac dogged her footsteps. "Hey! How about supper? We can order another pizza."

"No." The more Tina thought about what she was planning, the more difficult it was to stay convinced she was doing the right thing. Steeling herself against Zac's predictable negative reaction, she paused and faced him. "I want my eight days. All of them."

"Sure. No problem. I won't press you."

"Starting now." Not totally conscious of her actions, Tina swayed toward him slightly. Before she could right herself and make him understand exactly what she was trying to say, Zac reacted by taking her in his arms once more.

She closed her eyes and rested her hands flat on his chest. The rapid pounding of his heartbeat was echoed by an intense, throbbing pulse in her temples. No matter how much she wanted to be with him, she knew she couldn't stand a whole week of this kind of hopeless yearning. Neither could Zac. If they were together, he'd begin to ask questions—questions she wasn't ready to answer. The only sensible thing to do was insist he leave her alone.

Was there any chance Esther Fitch might take pity on her and back off? Tina wondered. Probably not, unless the Lord intervened to soften the woman's heart. Tina knew that in answer to prayer, God could do anything He wanted. However, she also knew that believers who'd been forgiven still had to accept the consequences of their mistakes. Chastisement, even when it was well deserved, was one of the hardest lessons to accept.

Tina exerted a light pressure on Zac's chest, and he loosened his hold. She eased away so he wouldn't think she was asking for another kiss when she tilted her head back to look up at him.

"I think we should give ourselves time apart to cool off and think this through," she said softly. "I have something important to tell you. Then, if you still want to marry me..."

"What do you mean, 'if' I still want to marry you?" A deep scowl creased his forehead. "Why should I change my mind?"

She saw the skeptical look on Zac's face begin to include a trace of annoyance. Well, too bad. It was probably foolish of her to dream that their love was ever going to have a chance to bloom and grow, anyway, given all the obstacles she'd brought along. Yet she couldn't help hoping they'd find some way to make the relationship work.

There were certainly a lot of "ifs" standing in the way. If Esther chose to keep silent, Tina would have to decide how much to reveal to Zac—and if it was fair to accept his marriage proposal. However, if she put off telling him anything until after Esther started spreading rumors, as she'd threatened, he'd be deeply hurt.

On the other hand, Tina knew that if she told him more than she needed to, he might leap to her defense, take her side against Craig, reveal the whole story and ruin more innocent lives back in California. Zac had a strong sense of right and wrong. She admired that fine quality in him.

It also scared her silly.

Sunday dawned bright and beautiful. Tina wasn't impressed. Scrunching down in bed she pulled the coverlet over her face to hide from the rays of sunshine streaming through her bedroom window.

Zorro batted at a partially exposed wisp of hair that trailed over her pillow. Getting no response, he gave up, jumped silently to the floor and began to chase the dust motes swirling in the sunbeams.

Tina felt his weight leave the bed. She peeked out, saw what he was doing and groaned. Must be nice to be a house cat, she mused. No responsibilities. No cares. Just eat, sleep and play. What a life. And what a contrast to her present disconcerting existence.

Lucky for them, cats had no conscience. She, on the other hand, could hardly wait to go back to work on Monday so she'd have something to do aside from fret about Zac. No matter how many times she rehearsed the story she planned to tell him, it never sounded plausible.

She would come across as a complete fool unless she mentioned having been her brother's legal guardian and then explained why she'd felt such a strong responsibility for his foolish actions. But if she went into detail about Craig's guilt, there was no way she could continue to shield him. He now had a family, a good job, and was leading a productive life. That was important. It meant her sacrifice had paid off, even if the cost had been far higher than she'd imagined. No way was she going to place him in jeopardy if she could help it.

Poor Craig. This time, he deserved her loyalty. And this time she wasn't sure how she was going to deliver it.

Hoping a hot shower would stimulate her weary brain, Tina got up and padded to the bathroom. This was Sunday. If she skipped Sunday School and church, she'd regret it all week. On the other hand, if she stayed for the main service and happened to run into Zac, it would be more than merely tough to ignore him. It would be impossible. She was already getting a familiar knot in her stomach every time she pictured his handsome face. Reality was bound to be worse. Much worse.

"I don't *want* to be in love!" Tina shouted. Her protest bounced off the bathroom walls and dissipated down the narrow hallway.

Turning on the shower full force, she stepped into the stinging spray. To her chagrin, she realized she didn't want to go to church, either.

Duty won out. Tina was arranging the crayons and pages to color when her first Sunday School students arrived. Little Connie Cain was holding the hand of a red-haired girl Tina didn't recognize. She was so busy making the new child feel at home, she didn't notice Justin at first. When she looked up, he was standing by the open door, staring at his shoes and kicking an invisible object on the rug.

It took her a few seconds to catch her breath and convince her hammering heart that Zac was nowhere to be seen. Relieved, she said, "Hi, Justin. Come on in and have a seat. We do things a lot like your other school does, so you already know my rules."

He didn't move. He also didn't look at her.

"Justin?" Tina approached and cautiously touched his shoulder. "Are you okay, honey?"

He shook his head. She crouched down to be on the same level. "What's the matter?"

Sniffling, he wiped away a tear with his pudgy fist. "I'm sorry, Miss Tina."

"For what? You didn't do anything wrong, did you?"

"Uh-huh." Starting to cry in earnest, he threw his arms around her neck, nearly toppling her.

Tina hugged and soothed him until she sensed he was calm enough to explain. Then she held him away so she could see his face, and dried his tears with a tissue, ending at his nose. "Here— Blow. That's better. Now, can you tell me what upset you so much?"

"It's all my fault," the boy said with a shuddering breath. "I...I didn't mean to make you mad."

"Oh, honey," Tina said lovingly. "I'm not mad at you. Why would I be?"

"Your Popsicle. I messed it up."

"It just melted, that's all," she assured him. "They're made out of ice. They're supposed to do that." Judging by his pained expression, the boy was not fully convinced, so she added, "If they didn't melt, we couldn't eat them."

"But...but you left. And you didn't come back."

Tina drew him to her in a motherly embrace, kissed his damp cheek and smoothed back his hair. "Oh, baby. I'm the one who's sorry. I should have told you goodbye before I went home. Of course I'm not mad at you." Unshed tears misted her vision. "You're very special to me."

"My daddy says you're crazy," he told her solemnly. "But I don't care. I love you, anyway."

Before she straightened, she paused long enough to smile at him and quietly whisper, "I love you, too."

The little boy beamed with delight. "Will you come over and play with me?"

"I'm pretty busy today," Tina hedged. "But you'll see me in regular preschool tomorrow."

Justin began to pout. "Daddy says he has to drive me. I want to go with you, like always."

"I don't see any problem with that," she agreed, finishing her classroom preparation while they talked. "As soon as Sunday School is over, I'll go find your father and tell him I'll be glad to keep taking you. How's that?''

From the doorway came a familiar, deep voice. "Why not tell me now?''

Every fine hair on Tina's arms prickled and stood on end at the sound of Zac's voice. Her heart flipped, then seemed to lodge in her suddenly constricted throat. She spun around to face him, barely managing to control her instinctive urge to flee. If he hadn't been blocking her escape, she might have given the concept more serious consideration.

Instead, she stood tall, her chin jutting out, and faced him. "Fine. I'll be happy to take Justin to pre-school with me in the morning, as always. There. How was that?''

"Well done. Quite explicit,'' Zac said.

"Good.'' There was one more question she felt compelled to ask. "Why would you assume I'd stop taking him?''

Zac shrugged. "I don't know. I don't seem to be able to tell *what* you're going to do or say, so I thought it would be best to prepare him, just in case. I didn't want him to be disappointed if you didn't show up tomorrow.''

"Did you really think I'd purposely disappoint an innocent, little boy? I would *never* do that. *Never.*'' It had gotten so quiet behind her, she knew she had the complete attention of every four-year-old in the small room.

Nodding slowly, Zac flashed a wry, lopsided grin.

"In that case, I have only two more things to say to you, Miss Tina."

"What two things?" She eyed him with suspicion.

"I wish I were a lot shorter...and about thirty years younger."

The endearing smile on his handsome face tied Tina's stomach in a knot the size of a beach ball. Nevertheless, she managed to reply, "If you were thirty years younger, Mr. Frazier, we wouldn't be having this conversation in the first place."

"That's probably true. Tell you what, Justin and I will save you a place so you can sit by us during church." Zac looked hopeful.

"Thanks, but I won't be staying today. I just came to teach my class. I'm going home right afterward."

That said, she boldly closed the classroom door to shut him out, and turned her attention back to the children.

Chapter Fourteen

The first hint of trouble came the following day. At first, Tina assumed her preschool classes were smaller because some of the children were sick. It wasn't unusual for germs to make the rounds, especially among the youngest students. Chickenpox was noted for its yearly attacks on any kids who hadn't already been exposed.

Monday, two were absent. Tuesday, it was five. By Thursday, Justin and Tommy were the only ones who showed up, and Tina's reasoning powers began to work overtime. Common childhood diseases all had specific incubation times, which tended to stagger the absences. When the first batch of kids was getting well, the second was just coming down with it, and so on. Even colds and flu didn't spread instantly.

So far, she hadn't heard any rumors pertaining to

herself. Then again, she wouldn't, would she. That was the insidious nature of gossip. It skipped the very people who *should* be told what was being said behind their backs so that they could refute it.

Pensive, Tina sighed. Justin and Tommy were playing peacefully on the rug by the toy shelves, and since her class had dwindled, she had no pressing duties. She eyed the nursery door. It was time to go and have a talk with Mavis.

The older woman was sitting in a rocking chair with the Carter twins, cradling one in each arm and slowly rocking. When Tina entered, she looked up, smiled, and nodded toward a matching chair beside her.

Leaning close so she could speak without waking the babies, Tina said, "I need to talk to you about my class." Her heart began to race. "Do you know why so many kids are absent?"

"I've heard some silly gossip, but don't worry about it, dear. This, too, shall pass, as the Bible says. As soon as everybody realizes how foolish it is to believe vicious rumors, the children will be back. I can't imagine how it's gone this far. I mean, *you* with a prison record? That's absolutely unthinkable!"

Steeling herself for what she knew she must do, Tina mustered her courage. She laced her fingers together, squeezed tight and said simply, "It's true," and watched her boss's reaction. Doubt was followed by astonishment.

"What? How? When?" Grimacing, Mavis shook

her head. "I don't believe it. How could you do this to me? I trusted you!"

"I'm so sorry." Remorse weighed heavily on Tina's conscience. "It happened a long time ago." She paused. "You don't have to fire me. I'll go."

"I think that's best."

The twins were stirring, so Mavis got up to return them to their cribs. Tina heard her mumbling words that had probably never been heard in that establishment in all the years she'd owned it.

Tina followed to help her place the first twin in bed without waking the second one. When both babies were comfortably settled, Tina took Mavis aside and told her, "You've been wonderful to me. I never meant to hurt you or your business. I just wish there was some way I could make it up to you, fix things."

Mavis scowled. "I'm afraid it's too late for that. The damage is done."

"I know. I've been through this kind of thing before, in other towns. Look at all the kids who are being kept home because of me. The situation won't get any better, either. It never does."

"I can't afford to wait and see."

"I know that, too." Tina started for the nursery door. "Can you get Vicki to come in to take my place this afternoon?"

"I'll get someone." Mavis accompanied Tina out of the nursery and closed the door behind them. "I wish there was another way to handle this."

"There isn't. Serenity is close-knit. People won't forget. That's why I need to leave."

"Leave this job, you mean?"

Standing tall, Tina accepted the inevitability of her choices. Slowly, sadly, she shook her head. "No. Not just the job. I need to leave town, too. Start over. Otherwise, I'll never be able to lead a normal life."

"Why didn't you tell me the whole truth in the first place?"

"Oh, sure. I apply for a job taking care of little kids, and before you even have a chance to get to know me or see how well I work, I tell you I have a prison record? I don't think so. In a big city they'd have done a background check on me first thing."

"So you came to a place like Serenity where we go on trust and our gut-feelings?"

"Yes." Tina sighed. "I hope you can forgive me."

"Was it very bad in prison?" Mavis asked.

"I got through it. That's all that matters." Tina smiled wistfully. "And just between you and me, I wasn't guilty in the first place."

"Then why..."

"It's a long story."

"Shorten it," Mavis ordered.

Pensive, Tina slowly shook her head. "The whole thing sounds so silly when I tell it. After my parents were killed in a car accident, I applied for custody of my younger brother, Craig. He was a real handful. I guess he was mad at the world, me included."

"That's understandable, losing his folks and all."

"I know. That's why I cut him so much slack, I suppose. Anyway, I'd loaned him my car so he could take some friends out for pizza, and he got in a wreck. When he came running into the house, he was scared silly and babbling something about wanting me to say I'd been driving because he'd had a few beers with his friends."

"You didn't!"

"Unfortunately, I did," Tina replied. "Before I'd had a chance to ask Craig anything about the accident, the police burst in and started shouting at us. I didn't know what to do so I took the blame to protect my brother. At the time, I didn't know he'd driven away from the scene and made the crash a hit-and-run."

"But surely, when you found out…"

Tina sighed. "There's more. When they searched my car they found drugs." Noting Mavis's concern she quickly added, "No! They weren't mine. Craig's so-called buddies had stashed them in my car after the accident so they wouldn't get in trouble if they were caught by the police. I hired a lawyer, of course, but by that time, even he didn't believe I was innocent. If I had it all to do over again, I sure wouldn't sell my house to pay his exorbitant fee."

With a concerned smile Mavis relented and patted Tina's arm. "Oh, honey. I do believe you. You don't have to say any more."

"Thanks." Tina's thoughts turned to Zac Frazier.

It would be a minor miracle if he hadn't already heard the juicy gossip about her. She'd foolishly let nearly a week pass, hoping and praying Esther would have a change of heart and decide to keep quiet.

Had Zac seemed out of sorts when she'd stopped by to pick up Justin that morning? She didn't think so. That probably meant he hadn't yet heard. Tina shivered. He might have by now, though, meaning it could already be too late to salvage the touchy situation by confessing.

Oh, Father, she pled silently, *I love him. What am I going to do now?* No booming voice from heaven answered. Instead, she felt a strong compulsion to race to Zac's office—a compulsion she knew better than to deny.

It took Miss Vicki half an hour to respond to Mavis's harried call. The minute Tina saw her replacement walk in, she grabbed her purse and headed for her truck.

The only traffic light in Serenity was red when Tina hit the main crossroads. It seemed to take *hours* for the signal to change. With no special left-turn lane or green arrow to indicate right-of-way, she was stuck waiting until Inez's grandmother, Lillian, managed to pilot her old green Buick through the intersection. By that time, the light had switched to yellow.

Tina was too frantic to endure another whole cycle. She floored the gas and whipped left, making it through at the last minute. Getting to Zac had become an obsession, although she didn't know what she was going to do or say when she reached him. Her befuddled brain refused to concentrate enough to form even one coherent thought. Given the erratic way she was driving, she figured that was just as well. One crisis at a time was her limit.

Wheeling into the high school faculty parking lot, Tina found it crammed full. She simply gave up and abandoned her truck in the aisle nearest the main building. Zac's office had to be close to the reception area. If not, she knew Rosemary could tell her where to find him.

The office receptionist looked more surprised than happy, when Tina burst through the door. *She's heard,* Tina reasoned. *And if she knows...*

Forcing herself to slow down and take deep, calming breaths, Tina smiled and approached the counter that separated the public from the faculty and support staff. "Hi, Rosemary. I'm here to see Zac Frazier. Is he available?"

"No. He's with a parent."

"That's okay." She sat down on the padded bench beneath the window. "I don't mind waiting."

"His appointment may take a long time. Could be hours."

Tina set her jaw and folded her arms across her chest in a pose of defiance. Her eyes narrowed. "I'll wait."

The other woman shrugged. "Have it your way."

Have it *my* way? Tina mused. It would certainly be nice to feel that normal for a change, wouldn't it? She shook her head slowly, thoughtfully. Given the defensive way she'd been forced to conduct herself lately, would she even recognize a normal life if she saw it?

Yes, if she remembered her family the way they were before she'd been left alone to raise Craig. At nineteen, she'd had no idea how to cope with a precocious sixteen-year-old. Poor Craig had been mad at the world. The last thing he'd wanted to do was allow his sister to discipline him, even though the courts had given her custody.

Tina closed her eyes and breathed a sigh. Thank God, Craig hadn't killed anyone when he'd wrecked her car! If he hadn't panicked and fled, he wouldn't have called undue attention to himself and nothing more would have come of it. But he ran. Like the kid he was. *And I took the blame because I was supposed to be in charge.*

The hands on the large, black-rimmed clock on the wall ticked off the minutes while Tina waited. She watched the red second hand jerk its way around the full three-hundred-and-sixty degrees, then do it again and again. If she hadn't been so worried about facing Zac, she might have been lulled into boredom. Instead, she remained so alert that she bolted off the bench every time anyone entered the reception area.

Finally, in the distance, she heard Zac's warm, familiar voice. He'd apparently opened the door to his private office while bidding someone goodbye. Tina smoothed her skirt and nervously tucked the sides of her long hair neatly behind her ears. Soon, she'd know if she was too late. One look at his face and she'd be able to tell.

A couple she recognized from church came around the corner ahead of Zac. When the husband nodded to her, his wife jabbed him in the ribs with her elbow. They hurried past without speaking. Tina hardly noticed. She had eyes for only one person, and he was gazing at her the way a thirsty, desert traveler stares at an oasis.

Tina quickly approached. "Don't worry. Justin's fine. I thought maybe you and I could talk, if you have a few minutes free."

"I'll make time," Zac said. He ushered Tina straight to his office, placed a chair for her, and perched on the edge of his desk next to it, grinning expectantly. "Well? Are you ready to give me an answer? I know the eight days aren't quite up yet, but..."

Tina didn't sit down. Instead, she eased close enough to lay a finger across his lips. "Shh. Let me do the talking. Please?"

Zac kissed her fingertips as he took her hand and held it. "No problem."

So much unrestrained emotion was coursing through her that she could hardly bear it. Oh, how she loved this dear man! He was strong and commanding, yet there was a gentle side to him, too. Her fondest hope was that his heart was also overflowing with compassion, because she was going to need all the forgiving he could muster.

Start with the most important thing, Tina told herself. Smiling through unshed tears she said, "I do love you, Zac."

"I love you, too." He was still holding her hand, and tried to pull her closer.

Tina resisted. "Wait. There's more."

"Nothing else matters," Zac said. "We love each other. We're both single and available. And Justin thinks you're almost as much fun as Max is."

She could tell by the pleased, confident look on his face that he expected her to laugh at that final observation. Instead, she sobered. "You don't know as much about me as you do about that stray dog."

Zac wouldn't give up. "I know you're a lot cuter than he is. Your long hair is prettier, too."

"This is serious. I'm trying to tell you something very important. Will you please stop kidding around?"

"I can't. I'm too happy." He raised one eyebrow as he continued to grin at her. "Guess you'll just have to muddle through as is."

Growing more and more frustrated, Tina threw her hands in the air and strode away from him, hoping distance might help her concentrate. It didn't. She was so flustered, she was ready to scream instead of making a sensible effort to salvage their floundering relationship.

Tears pooled behind her lashes. *Terrific.* Crying wasn't going to help one bit, and now she had *that* urge to deal with, too.

Fighting the impulse to give in to her turbulent emotions, Tina took a deep breath and faced Zac. "Okay. It started a long time ago, when I was nineteen. My—"

Zac interrupted. "Hey, I don't have to hear every detail. Make it easy on yourself. Just spit it out and get it over with."

"No. I have to make you understand, first."

"No, you don't." He was shaking his head and smiling benevolently. "There's nothing you can tell me that I haven't heard a thousand times in my job as a counselor."

He looked so open, so ready to accept whatever she said, that Tina's prior misgivings seemed suddenly foolish. She and Zac loved each other. She was about to ask him to take her just as she was. How could she not do the same for him?

"Okay," she began tentatively, "I have a record."

"I prefer CDs, myself. They sound better."

"No, Zac. A *record*. As in prison. I was charged with hit-and-run and drug possession and sentenced to three years."

He came off the edge of the desk with a lurch. "What?"

"I'd hoped nobody would find out. I wouldn't be telling you now if Esther Fitch hadn't threatened to expose me."

Zac was shaking his head, talking to himself and pacing in random circles. "That's impossible. You and that woman have nothing in common. Nothing!"

"Nothing but incarceration. That's where she and I met. We were in the same jail," Tina said. It was killing her to see him looking so disappointed. "I'm not proud of my past. It's just there. I can't change it. Or make it go away so it won't impact your career. That's one of the reasons I kept telling you I didn't want to get serious."

Still in shock, he stared at her. "My career?"

"Yes. That was why I asked if you were sure you wanted to be a youth minister."

"Ah, my career," Zac muttered.

Tina saw his eyes narrow, his jaw clench. Befuddlement was gone. Anger had taken its place.

"What about my *son?* Did you bother to think of him?"

"Of course I did!"

Shaking his head in evident disgust, Zac asked, "And what about everybody else's kids? How did you manage to get a job taking care of children?"

"Mavis didn't know. Not till this morning. I told her the truth just before I quit."

"So, I'm the last to hear?"

"Only because you aren't part of the town grapevine," Tina insisted. "Esther tried to blackmail me into doing her a favor. When I refused, she said she'd give me a week to change my mind. That was why

I asked you to wait eight days. Only, she lied. She must have started blabbing right after I left her."

"I heard there was no honor among thieves."

"I'm not a thief!" Tina cried.

"Then, what are you?" Zac's harsh tone sounded almost menacing.

Tina had had enough. "I'm a fool!" she shouted. "A stupid, idiotic fool. I thought love would be enough."

"Love without honesty is worthless. A counterfeit. It's not even close to the real thing," he declared. "If you'd been as sincere as you claim, you'd have told me the truth up front, when it might have made a difference."

"Oh, it would have made a difference, all right. I learned *that* when I heard your expert opinion of Esther Fitch. The only mistake I made was not remembering how you felt." Whirling, Tina headed for the door.

"Where are you going? I'm not through."

"Oh, yes, you are." She jerked open the door and made a dash for her truck.

The outburst of hysterical weeping didn't seize her until she was halfway home.

If her emotions hadn't been so raw, Tina would have stopped at the preschool to speak to Justin that same afternoon. Because she didn't want to upset him, she decided to wait until her plans were firm before bidding him a final goodbye.

One of her first steps the following day was to visit the church and drop off the Sunday School teacher's guide and other materials for her class. She'd intended to slip in and out without having to speak to anyone. Unfortunately, one of the deacons was cutting the lawn when she got there. He waved, shut off the mower and started up the grassy slope to where she'd parked.

"Mornin' Tina."

"Good morning, Sam." Judging by the warm greeting, she suspected he hadn't heard. She climbed back into her truck. "Sorry I can't stop to talk. I've got a million things to do today."

He removed his cap and mopped his brow with a bandanna. "I heard you was movin'. That's a shame, you ask me. You've been real good for this church, no matter what they say."

Tina was flabbergasted. "You *know?*"

"About your trouble? Shoot, everybody does. I just don't understand why you don't hang around and let all the hoo-haw die down. This ain't a bad place to live. Them that talk the worst about others are usually the ones with the most secrets of their own to hide." He chuckled. "I could tell you a few wild tales, that's a fact."

"Well, don't," Tina said, finally breaking into a smile. "I've had enough stories told about me to know what kind of trouble gossip can cause. I suppose that's why the scriptures list it right up there with murder."

"Prob'ly so." Sam touched the brim of his cap and backed away. "You take care, Miss Tina. You'll be sorely missed around here."

"Thanks. It's sweet of you to say that. I'll miss this place, too."

"You can always come on back."

Her smile waned. "No. I'm afraid that's one thing I've learned the hard way, Sam. What's done is done. We can never go back and undo anything."

"Well..." His grin spread to crinkle his sun-weathered skin and light the eyes below his bushy gray brows. "Just remember, nobody's perfect. If it wasn't for Jesus takin' care of our sins, we'd *all* be in deep...manure."

Tina couldn't help smiling at his candid observation. "Maybe you should get up and preach next Sunday's sermon, Sam. I've never heard forgiveness explained so clearly."

Chapter Fifteen

Tina made arrangements with her landlord to leave most of her furniture behind in exchange for a month's rent. Considering where she was planning to go first, she didn't know how long it would be until she decided to set up housekeeping again.

She hadn't seen Zac for days. That was just as well. It was Justin she needed to talk to, not his father. Keeping careful watch on the Frazier house, she finally saw the little boy come outside to play with his dog.

Max saw her first and greeted her through the chain-link fence as if she were a long-lost buddy. Justin, however, was not as sure of himself. Silent and still, he stared up at Tina.

"I came to talk to you," she whispered. "Can you leave the dog in there and come out here for a second?"

He cast a wary look toward the house. "I guess so."

"Good." As soon as he joined her, she crouched down to be on his level and took his hands. "I didn't want to leave without saying goodbye."

"Leave?" His high voice trembled.

"I'm moving away," Tina explained.

"No!" It was more a wail than a word. He launched his little body at her, wrapped both arms around her neck, buried his face against her neck and began to cry.

Tina's eyes were filled with tears, too. She held him close and rocked gently, patting his back and making soothing noises. As soon as he'd calmed down some, she said, "Shush, baby. It's okay. I'll miss you bunches, too. I'd like to stay here but I just can't. Someday, when you're older, you'll understand."

He sniffled and lifted his face to look at her as he asked solemnly, "Are...are you gonna die like my mommy?"

The poignant question fractured her heart into a million pieces. "Oh, Justin, no. I'll be living someplace else, that's all. Why would you think I was going to die?"

"When I ask about my mommy, Daddy always says I'll understand when I'm older."

Of course. His mother had left him suddenly, unexplainably, and now Tina was about to do the same thing. To a child, the comparison of the two events made perfect sense.

"Tell you what," Tina said, trying to sound joyful. "I have your telephone number. I promise I'll call you from wherever I am, just so you'll know I'm all right. Would you like that?"

"Uh-huh." The sound of a banging door came from the direction of his house, making Justin jump.

Tina quickly straightened. With Max standing guard on the opposite side of the fence and directing his undivided attention toward his young master, there was no way Zac could keep from noticing. Therefore, unless she wanted to undergo another inquisition—or worse—she'd better head for home.

"Okay," Tina whispered hoarsely. "It's a deal, but it'll have to be our special secret." She laid her index finger across her lips. "No fair telling. Promise?"

In the distance, Zac began calling to Justin. Eyes wide, the boy whirled. Tina backed away as she said, "Go on, honey, before you get in trouble."

"But…"

She darted back to place a quick kiss on the child's forehead and give him a parting hug. "I'll call you. I promise. Cross my heart."

"Lots of times?" he asked, sounding lost and insecure.

"If that's what you want." She ducked around the nearest shrubbery to hide. "Now go on. Scoot."

Waiting behind the overgrown hedge, Tina

watched the little boy slip through the gate and heard him answer his father. In seconds, Zac had scooped the boy up in his arms and was carrying him back toward the house.

Peeking over his father's shoulder, Justin smiled and waved a private goodbye, then mimicked her sign of secrecy by placing a finger against his lips.

Tina bit her lower lip. When she'd decided to give up Zac she'd consoled herself with the assurance that she was acting for his ultimate good. Until this moment, she'd believed that nothing else she ever did would hurt as much as that had. She'd been mistaken. The sight of him carrying that dear little boy away from her for the last time caused such agony of spirit that she had to clench her fists and clamp her jaw shut to keep from crying out.

The monumental effort stole her breath and overwhelmed her mind. She wanted to weep, to wail, to frantically beat her fists against the ground and scream at God for letting her fall in love with Zac and his son in the first place, yet she was too numbed by grief to do any of those things.

Instead, she slowly made her way home and continued to pack without caring what she took or what she left behind. Material possessions no longer mattered. Nothing did.

Zac was at work when Tina threw the last of her belongings into her truck and left Serenity for good. His first clue that she'd actually moved was a call from her landlord asking him if he wanted to rent her house because it had a much nicer yard. That's when reality set in.

He pushed back from his desk and stared, unseeing, at the office wall. Tina was gone. Really gone. It seemed unbelievable. All his favorite memories of Serenity included her. Like it or not, that woman had become an integral part of his life. And of Justin's.

Thinking about her, remembering their time together, made him happy, and exasperated, and melancholy, all at the same time—a confusing condition that didn't help foster an amiable disposition.

His unexpected encounter with Esther Fitch in the school parking lot later that afternoon capped the dismal day. If she hadn't accosted him, Zac gladly would have passed her by without speaking.

"Did she tell you all about it?" Esther jockeyed to block his way and stood firm.

"If you want to see me, Mrs. Fitch, you need to make an appointment. I should have a little time later in the week."

"It's not my fault, what happened," Esther insisted, ignoring his formal manner. "I told her I'd keep my mouth shut, but oh, no, she had to get on her high horse about it. I just want to make sure you're not blaming my poor Bennie."

Zac took a deep, settling breath before chancing to speak. "Blaming him for what?"

"For runnin' your girlfriend out of town. All she'd

of had to do was one little favor for me and nobody'd have been the wiser about her past."

Had Tina mentioned something about Esther wanting a favor? He wasn't sure. At the time, he'd been so shocked that he hadn't been able to focus on her confession enough to ask for details. Now, he wished he had.

Clenched fists were the only outward sign of Zac's roiling emotions as he asked, "What kind of a favor?"

"For Bennie, of course."

The woman was giving him a look that plainly said she thought he was dumber than dirt. Zac didn't care. Rather than guess what she'd done to Tina, he wanted her to spell it out. "What does Ms. Braddock have to do with Bennie?"

"Not her. *You!* All she'd of had to do was talk to you. Get you to bend a little. Give my son a break. It's not like I was wanting a lot." She snorted derisively.

Zac's voice was gruff. "Tina refused?"

"Right off. Wouldn't listen to reason. Gave me some stupid line about honesty and Bennie needing to take the blame himself when he failed."

"You should have listened to her. She was right. The more you keep trying to bail your son out of trouble, the harder it will be for him to learn how to function as a responsible adult."

"I love my boy!" Esther insisted. "I may not be

much, in your eyes, but I'm his mother and I love him.''

"I can see that, Mrs. Fitch. The question is, do you want him to stand on his own someday, or wind up following in your footsteps because you taught him how easy it can be to cheat the system?''

Her response was pretty much as he'd expected. Muttering curses, she turned and stalked away.

Zac shook his head slowly, sighed, and started for his car while he mulled over the importance of what he'd just learned. Tina could have prevented her own exposure by simply lying and trying to manipulate him, yet she'd risked everything and refused because she'd felt it was the right thing to do. That kind of pure integrity was rare. To find it in a person who had served time in prison...

And he'd been so hardheaded that he'd driven her away. Instead of accepting Tina, faults and all, he'd judged her without giving her a chance to explain. The fact that she'd kept him in the dark, at first, had bruised his male pride, and he'd retaliated without even realizing what he was doing until it was too late. Maybe Esther Fitch's unspoken opinion was right. Maybe he *was* dumber than dirt.

But maybe it wasn't too late! "I'll crawl if I have to,'' Zac told himself as he drove toward the day care center to pick up Justin. "I don't care what Tina did in the past. I'll find her and keep apologizing until she gives me—gives us—another chance.''

That decision lifted his spirits enough that he actually smiled for the first time in longer than he cared to admit.

By that evening, Zac was down in the dumps again. He'd figured Mavis would know where Tina had gone, but she was as much in the dark as everyone else he talked to. He was rapidly running out of people to ask.

Well, at least Justin isn't depressed, Zac thought, watching his son push a toy car across the floor while making noises like a motor. The kid was as energetic and cheerful as ever—maybe more so. He hadn't wanted to go outside to play that evening the way he usually did, but that was understandable since the late summer heat lingered until sundown. Other than that, Justin's behavior seemed perfectly normal. He'd obviously adjusted to Tina's absence a lot better than his daddy had.

Zac was in the kitchen fixing supper, when the telephone rang. Before he could reach it, Justin had answered and was already saying, "Hello?"

"I'll take that." Zac held out his hand.

The boy refused to relinquish the receiver. "Hello? Hello?" he repeated.

Zac pried the phone from his fingers and listened. A recorded, computerized sales spiel was just beginning. Disgusted, Zac slammed down the receiver and headed back to the kitchen. Behind him, Justin started to wail.

That unexpected reaction tempered Zac's grumpy

disposition. "You know I've told you not to answer the phone. I'm not mad at you for doing it this time, if that's what you're upset about. I'm mad at the people who call us and try to sell us something right at supper time."

Surprisingly, the explanation didn't begin to halt Justin's emotional outburst, so Zac crouched down to reassure him. "Hey. I'm not mad at you, okay? Honest, I'm not. I know I've been kind of short-tempered, lately. I'm sorry if I scared you." He patted the boy's back as he spoke. "Just don't forget the rules and answer the phone again. Okay?"

All he got out of Justin was more shuddering sobs, so he took him by the hand and led him to the bathroom where he helped him blow his nose and washed his face with cool water. "There. Isn't that better? Now—"

In the other room, the telephone started to ring. Justin bolted from his father's grasp and dashed down the hall. Zac went after him. When he reached the living room, he found Justin hiding behind the sofa. He had dragged the telephone back there with him!

Zac peered over the couch. "Hey, buddy, what are you doing down there?"

Justin's shoulders slumped as he hung up the receiver, got to his feet and returned the phone to the side table. "Nothin'."

"Who was that?"

"Just some man."

"Who did you *think* it might be?" Zac asked. He was beginning to suspect why his son hadn't wanted to go out and play before supper lately. And why he hadn't once lamented the fact that Miss Tina was gone. The child's subsequent refusal to answer was further proof. "Justin..." he said coaxingly, "tell Daddy what's going on."

The boy shook his head energetically and stared down at his shoes.

Zac took his hand, led him around to an easy chair, sat down and lifted him into his lap. "Okay. You can keep your secret if you want to."

"I can?" Justin whispered.

"Yes, you can. And I'll do the talking for you if you're out playing or something when Miss Tina calls."

"No!" He tried to wiggle free and jump down, but he was being held too securely.

"Don't you want me to talk to her?" Zac asked with careful nonchalance.

"No. She promised she'd call *me*."

Nodding, Zac said, "Uh-huh. I thought so." Justin continued to squirm, so he turned him loose. "Do you know where Tina went, son?"

"She moved away."

"I know that. I mean, did she happen to say where she was going?"

"No." Pouting, the child stared up at his father, then glanced over at the silent telephone.

"Well, don't worry," Zac reassured him. "I won't

spoil your talk with Miss Tina. You can answer the phone anytime it rings. But if the call is for me, you have to promise to come get me right away. How does that sound?''

''Fine!''

''Then, it's settled.'' He crossed to the window and began to shift furniture around. ''Look. I have an idea. If we open the front window and set the phone right here on the sill, you can go out and play with Max and you'll still hear it if it rings. I won't answer it, I promise.''

''All right!'' Justin galloped out the door with a whoop.

''One more thing,'' Zac muttered to himself. Reaching for the telephone directory and flipping it open to the front pages, he dialed, then waited impatiently until a young voice answered, ''Customer service. How may I help you?''

''I want to order Caller ID,'' Zac said. ''I don't care what it costs. And I need it *yesterday*.''

Tina called Justin three days later, on a Sunday afternoon. Zac didn't have to hear her name to know who it was. The delight in his son's expression and the way he held the receiver so tightly told Zac everything.

''I did go to Sunday School,'' the boy said. ''Yeah. It was okay. I miss you.''

Imagining the other side of the conversation and picturing Tina, Zac sighed.

"I'm fine. He's okay, too." Justin looked up at his father, then said, "Yeah. He's right here." There was a long pause. "No. He's not mad at me. I think he misses you, too."

It was hard for Zac to keep from shouting confirmation. Afraid that any such outburst might cause Tina to hang up, he held his tongue. He'd encouraged his son to pose some leading questions when he finally talked to her. He just hoped the boy remembered.

"Do you have a nice house?" Justin asked, listening carefully. Then he said, "Maybe I could come visit you. Is it far?"

The way his expression sobered when he said "Oh," told Zac she hadn't provided an invitation.

"My dad could drive me," the boy offered, sounding hopeful. Then he asked, "Why not? Oh. I thought you kind of liked him. He likes you."

Zac was pacing, praying Tina would listen to the child's simple wisdom. Even if she never forgave him and they didn't wind up becoming a family, he needed to see her face-to-face. To tell her how wrong he'd been, how truly sorry he was. To convince her he didn't care what she'd done in the past—he loved her, anyway. Just as she was.

"Okay. Bye," the boy said sadly. He hung up and turned to his father. "Did I do okay?"

"You did fine," Zac told him with a pat on the head. "It's not your fault Tina left us. I'm the one who made all the mistakes. I'm really sorry, buddy."

Justin hugged his leg the way he had when they'd first come to Serenity and he'd felt so insecure. "It's okay."

"What did she say about me?" Zac asked, almost afraid to hear the answer.

The boy straightened and shrugged. "Nothin'."

"How about when you told her I liked her? What did she say then?" Zac leaned over the small, black Caller ID box he'd had installed and started to write down the number. No wonder it had taken so long for her to call. Judging by the area code, she'd traveled all the way to Southern California.

"I don't know," Justin said.

"Why not? You just talked to her a second ago." Though he was at his wits' end, Zac managed to maintain a calm, even tone for the boy's sake. Heaven help any parents who tried to carry on a logical, meaningful conversation with their four-year-old!

"'Cause."

Zac tried once more. "Because *why?*"

"'Cause Miss Tina was cryin' too hard. I couldn't hardly understand her." Justin gave his father a curious look that indicated he was surprised it had taken a grown-up so long to figure things out.

"Crying? She was?" Awed by the possible implications, Zac couldn't keep the joy out of his voice. "All right!"

Justin blinked and stared at him. "Is that good?"

"It's wonderful," Zac shouted, scooping him up

in his arms and whirling around and around till they were both so dizzy they collapsed on the sofa together.

Zac caught his breath, his heart pounding with anticipation, and reached over to pat Justin on the leg. "How would you like to fly in an airplane?"

"A jet?"

"Well, not a fighter plane like you see in the movies, but the trip will still be fun."

"Where are we going?"

Zac thought about the phone number he'd jotted down. If he couldn't get the address information he needed from the Internet, he might have to call a friend in law enforcement for help, and that would take longer. One thing was certain. If he didn't find out where Tina was and go after her soon, she might move again and disappear for good. He couldn't let that happen. Even if taking unscheduled time off cost him his current job.

"I'm not quite sure yet." Zac purposely hedged, not wanting Justin to accidentally give away their plans if Tina called again before they left. "I have a few arrangements to make first."

"Can we go camping in the van, too?"

"No. We'll have to leave that parked at the airport for when we come back." A comical scenario popped into Zac's head, and he laughed as he ruffled the boy's dark hair. "Tell you what. We'll take along our sleeping bags. How's that?" He could picture

Tina opening her front door some morning and finding them camped on her lawn!

"Yeah!" Justin hollered.

It was all Zac could do to contain the same feeling of elation. This whole idea kept getting better and better.

The name Braddock was not associated with the west coast address Zac finally acquired. Confused, he still had to follow the only lead he had. If it turned out to be a dead end, he'd come home and try again until he located Tina—or ran out of money trying.

Justin slept during the flight and most of the ride through the San Gabriel Valley to their destination, a modest tract house in Arcadia, California.

Slowing the rental car, Zac cruised past the address, trying to decide if he should call first or go knock on the door. He opted for the element of surprise. That way, if Tina *was* there, she wouldn't have a chance to run.

Nervous as a teenager on his first date, Zac pulled into the driveway of the strange house. He'd been rehearsing what he intended to say to Tina ever since he'd decided to find her, but all of a sudden the pat phrases seemed trite. Any words of wisdom he'd managed to come up with on his own were gone, too, floating off into oblivion like the fragile soap bubbles Justin liked to blow.

Zac found a shady place to park right next to the small porch, so he temporarily left his sleeping son in the car, its windows rolled down, when he went to the door. The screen was closed, but the door itself was open. He decided to call out rather than ring the bell.

"Hello. Anybody home?"

A small, red-haired child of about three peeked around a corner, then ducked out of sight. In seconds, a young woman carrying a baby against her chest in a blue canvas sling came to the door. "Yes? Can I help you?"

"I hope so," Zac said. "I'm looking for Tina Braddock."

"I'm sorry, there's... Wait a minute. Stay right there," she said. "I'll be right back."

Zac fidgeted. *It was the wrong house*. Dejected beyond belief, he started back to the car.

He was reaching for the door handle when a familiar voice said, "I'm not Tina Braddock. My real name is Christina Ferguson."

Zac whirled. It was her! It was really her!

"Around here they call me Chris," she explained. "My brother's name is Craig. When we were kids we were always called Chris and Craig, probably because those names sounded so good together."

Speechless, Zac stared. She'd cut her long hair. The new style made her look thinner, younger somehow. There was also sadness in her eyes. "I...I thought I had the wrong house," he stuttered.

"You do. You shouldn't have come."

"You shouldn't have left us," he countered.

"You know very well why I had to." Tina began to scowl at him. "What *are* you doing here?"

Zac approached cautiously, hoping she wouldn't slam the door in his face before he had a chance to tell her how he felt. "I came to apologize to you," he said. "I shouldn't have lost my temper. I was wrong."

She agreed with him. "Yes, you were."

Beginning to smile with relief, he noted that she, too, was having trouble remaining emotionally distant. "Okay. That's a start. How long do you think it may take you to forgive me for being such a jerk?"

"You're already forgiven," Tina told him softly. Instead of resisting when Zac opened the screen door, she stepped out and joined him on the porch. "But that doesn't change anything. I'm still not going back to Serenity."

He laid his hands gently on her shoulders and felt her tremble at the touch. "Fine. We'll start over someplace else. Get new jobs. I'll probably be fired, anyway."

"Fired? Why?" Looking into his eyes, she was so overcome by deep, passionate emotion that she barely heard him reply.

"Because I took an unscheduled leave to chase after the woman I love."

It took a moment for his statement to sink in. Tina gasped, her mouth agape. She finally managed to squeak, "Me? You still love me? Even now?"

Zac was so overjoyed to have found her that he felt light-headed. "I always said you were smart."

"Stop teasing. I'm not smart. If I were, I'd never have gotten sent to jail in the first place."

"True. But whatever you did, I can tell you're totally honest now, and that's what counts. Whatever mistakes you made years ago shouldn't change how I feel about you. Not as long as you've totally reformed."

Tina stiffened. "Yes, they should."

"Why? There's no question that you've turned your whole life around. And you certainly don't brag about being in prison or carry on the way Mrs. Fitch does."

"But...you saw what happened when the people in Serenity found out about me."

"No," Zac said, shaking his head. "All I saw was the beginning of a good lesson in loving one another, no matter what. When you ran away, you ended it before most folks had learned what I think the Lord was trying to teach them." He bent and kissed her parted lips to silence her before she could argue.

Tina slid her arms around his neck and kissed him back. Confusion reigned in her heart and mind. Could Zac be right? Was it conceivable that the Lord could actually use her terrible past to His advantage? Of *course* He could! She'd just never opened her mind enough to consider that possibility before.

She stared up at the man who had accepted her without condemnation, even though she hadn't loved him enough to trust him to do so. When he whispered, "Marry me, Tina?" she felt as if she were floating a hundred feet off the ground.

Could this be happening? Was she finally free to follow her desires and accept the blessings God offered—without hesitation, without guilt and without reservation?

"You're sure?" she asked, her voice barely audible.

"I'm sure." Zac cupped her face in his hands and gazed down at her with pure, unquestioned love. "Was that a *yes?*"

"Yes!" was all she managed to say, before Zac grabbed her and kissed her breathless. When they came up for air, she planted her palms flat on his chest and gave a halfhearted push. "Wait. You have to listen to me."

"Not if you plan to change your mind," he said, leaning down to reclaim her lips. "I don't think I could stand it if you did that."

Tina caressed his cheek and smiled. "I'm not going to change my mind. Ever. I just want you to know the truth about why I went to prison. Let me tell you? Please?"

His slight nod gave her the go-ahead, and she explained how she'd been made her brother's guardian, how she'd felt responsible for his mistakes, and how she'd taken the punishment meant for him.

When she saw anger start to color Zac's expression, she added, "Don't blame Craig. The accident was his fault, but my involvement, afterward, was strictly my own stupid decision. By the time I realized I'd done the wrong thing and tried to take back my confession, it was too late. No one believed me. Not even my lawyer."

"Your brother walked off scot-free?"

"Not exactly." Tina flashed a satisfied grin. "Craig's whole life changed because of that accident. He turned back to the Christian faith he'd had as a child, cleaned up his act, finished school and built a good life. He has a wonderful wife and two great kids. That's why I've never tried to clear my name. I can't take the chance he'd be sent to prison and lose everything he's worked so hard for."

She took Zac's hand and squeezed affectionately. "This is Craig's house. Come on. I want you to meet everybody. And remember what you told me about forgiveness. Craig needs it as much as I did. He's even offered to go back to Serenity with me, stand up in a town meeting and admit his guilt."

"Well, that's better. When?"

"Never. I told him to forget it. He's already made full restitution to the man he hurt in the car accident. That's enough for me."

Zac raised an eyebrow but refrained from telling her that it wasn't nearly enough for *him*. As he mulled over the situation, a plan started to take shape in his mind. If Tina's brother had meant it when he'd volunteered to speak out and clear her name, *somebody* should encourage him to go ahead and do it.

Since Tina wasn't willing to be that somebody, Zac knew it was up to him.

He turned toward the rental car. "Okay. I'll get Justin."

"Justin's *here?* Why didn't you tell me?" Thrilled, Tina dashed by him and jerked open the rear door.

The instant the little boy awoke, he recognized who was bending over him. Giving a happy shriek, he held out his arms to her. "Miss Tina!"

"Hi, sweetheart," she said, fighting tears of joy while she unfastened his seat belt. "I missed you."

"Me, too!" The child leaped into her arms and hugged her neck as if he never intended to let go.

Zac helped her straighten, still holding Justin, and enfolded both his son and his bride-to-be in a wide embrace.

Tina heard his voice break with emotion as he whispered, *"Thank you, God."*

Blessed beyond belief she added a heartfelt, "Amen."

Epilogue

Zac's private talk with Craig had gone well. So had the wedding plans. Although Zac would have preferred that he and Tina be married in their home church in Serenity, she was adamantly against it, so they'd settled on the small church where Craig and his family worshiped.

The ceremony was intimate. To Tina's delight and relief, Zac had asked Craig to be his best man even before she'd decided to make her sister-in-law matron of honor. Seeing the two men she loved most standing at the front of the sanctuary together, waiting for her to walk down the aisle, was wonderful. Almost as wonderful as becoming Zac's wife and Justin's mother.

Their honeymoon was necessarily short, which was just as well since they'd decided they should include Justin. Tina would never have agreed to go home to Serenity with Zac afterward if he hadn't convinced her he'd lose his job if he didn't return to work as soon as possible.

Filled with misgivings, she was unusually quiet during the drive north from the airport in Little Rock. Justin napped in the back seat of the van.

When they'd almost reached Serenity, Zac noticed that Tina was getting fidgety. He reached over and took her hand. "It'll be okay, honey. I'm right. You'll see."

"I wish I could believe you," she said softly. "It's never been okay before."

"Just remember, you can't expect to please everybody. No matter what we do or say, there's always someone who takes offense. That's part of living. We're not accountable to them. Our job is to stay true to the Lord and try to behave the way He'd want us to." Zac squeezed her fingers. "You're only responsible for what *you* do, honey. How other people respond is up to them."

"You mean 'Love one another...,' like it says in the thirteenth chapter of John?" Tina chewed her lower lip. "I don't know if I can do that, Zac. Some really awful things were said about me behind my back."

"And to your face, especially if you count me." He brought her hand to his lips and kissed her fingertips. "I'll never forgive myself for putting you through that."

"It's over." Tina's voice echoed the love and forgiveness in her heart.

"That's exactly what I've been trying to tell you for the past two weeks. It's all over. Now we start again. Together."

Turning north on highway sixty-two at Ash Flat, he began to grin.

Tina noticed immediately. "What are you smiling about?"

"Oh, nothing."

"Za-a-a-ac. I know you better than that. What have you got up your sleeve?"

"My arm?" He made a silly face as she gave him a playful whack on the shoulder. "Okay. We're almost there so I guess I should tell you. I bought us a house."

"A *what?*"

"We don't have to keep it if you don't like it. I got such a great deal on the place, I couldn't turn it down. You'll love the yard. It's got more flowers than I've ever seen in one place before. Used to be rented by a gardening nut who took off for California and left it vacant."

"My house?" Tina gasped. "You bought *my* house?"

"Sure did. I've had the Peterson kids looking after Max at my old place. And I hired them to water your yard while we were gone, too, so your plants should be in pretty good shape. I knew how much they meant to you."

"Oh, Zac..." She leaned as close as the separate front seats in his van would allow and laid her cheek on his shoulder. "You're so sweet."

"See that you remember that in the future," he cautioned. "Now, close your eyes. We're almost there."

"Why should I close my eyes?"

"Because your husband asked you to?"

Tina made a pouting face. "Okay. Since you put it that way. Don't make me keep them closed too long, though. I get dizzy on curves if I don't watch the road."

"Hang tough. Just a little farther." Pulling to a stop in front of their house, he saw the result of Craig's visit to Serenity while they'd been honeymooning. It was better than Zac had dared hope. Big yellow bows were tied on the porch posts and hung from every branch and stem strong enough to support them. Ladies from Tina's church had tables laden with food set up in the driveway.

"Can I look now?" Tina asked.

"Not yet. Stay right there. And don't peek." Zac circled the van, opened her door and helped her out. As soon as he'd turned her to face the unofficial welcoming committee, he said, "Okay. You can look."

Tina couldn't believe it. Dumbfounded, she pressed her fingertips to her lips and stared. So many folks had shown up to greet her that she couldn't count them all! Everybody was standing very still, apparently waiting for her to make the next move.

And grouped in the very front, holding hands, was her brother and his whole happy little family.

Blinking back tears of joy, Tina gazed up at Zac and slipped her arms around his waist. "You did this for me?"

"I can't take all the credit," he said. "Craig played a big part, too."

"Oh, Zac! You didn't let him—"

"Hush. No harm was done. I looked into it and found out the statute of limitations on his crime had run out. He's not in any danger of being arrested."

Tina was incredulous. "He's not?"

"No, he's not. And even if he were, he'd have come here and told the truth for your sake. He really is a straight-up guy. You should be proud of the way you raised him."

"Thanks. I did everything the hard way, though. I wish I had it all to do over again."

Zac laughed. "You will. Wait till Justin gets old enough to drive a car."

"Oh, dear... I hadn't thought about that. He's already a handful. I'll bet his teenage years will be awful."

"Maybe not. I'm hoping he'll want to set a good example for his younger brothers and sisters."

"What younger...?" Tina blushed. "Oh, *those* younger brothers and sisters. Well, before we can start to do anything about *that*..." She smiled and waved at the folks who'd been waiting for a sign that she'd forgiven them. "You'd better bring Justin and come on. We have company."

"A welcome home party seemed like a good idea when I thought of it," Zac said, lifting his son out of the van and falling into step beside her. "Only, I didn't dream half the town would show up!"

Laughing gaily and feeling as if the sun was shining more brightly than ever before, Tina approached the crowd and opened her arms wide to include everyone.

Craig ran to her first, his wife and children close behind, and gave her a bear hug. "Surprised?"

"Flabbergasted." She saw him offer his hand to Zac, saw them shake like brothers, and asked, "Okay. How long have you two been in cahoots?"

"Long enough," Craig said. "Zac made most of the local arrangements. Even convinced your pastor to let me speak from the pulpit and explain what kind of person you really are—" His voice broke. "And what you did for me."

Stepping between the two men, Tina slipped one arm around each of their waists and squeezed them tightly. "I was no hero, Craig. What I did was tell a lie that came back to bite me." Blinking back tears of joy and relief, she glanced up at her brother. "It was the stupidest thing I've ever done. But thanks for coming here like this and setting the record straight."

"You're welcome." He winked at Zac and added, "Besides, somebody had to drive your old truck home and get it out of my yard. My stuffy, citified neighbors were beginning to complain that it was a terrible eyesore.''

''Well, it fits in just fine around here,'' Tina said, gazing fondly up at her husband. ''And so do I...now.''

Zac kissed her forehead. ''You mean, you don't want to sell the house?''

Laughing lightly and standing on tiptoe to whisper in his ear, she told him, ''Nope. At least, not until we fill it up with children and run out of room.''

*　*　*　*　*

Dear Reader,

I've really struggled and prayed over what to say in this letter. If I were a perfect Christian, it would be easy.

Then again, if I were perfectly loving, the way Jesus commanded His disciples to be to each other in John 13:34, I might not have been able to create the characters and situations in this book.

When I was younger, I thought the Bible was like a textbook, full of rules to follow using my own willpower. Anyone who has tried to do that, without the help of the Holy Spirit, knows it's impossible. When I made the conscious decision to turn my life over to God, through Jesus Christ, and began to study with new insight, I realized that my rebirth as a true believer was just the beginning. I still had a *long* way to go!

My point is not that Christians are fallible, which we are, it's that once we've turned to Jesus, we're enrolled in God's school. Sometimes we do well. Sometimes we don't. But the Lord knows what's in our hearts, and with His help we will learn to love one another as He has loved us.

I'd love to hear from you! If you'd like a reply, please enclose a self-addressed, stamped envelope. Or look me up at http://www.centurytel.net/valeriewhisenand/ and read all about my upcoming books.

Blessings,

Valerie Hansen

Valerie Hansen, P.O. Box 13, Glencoe, AR 72539